AT THE CONFLUENCE

by Christopher K. Doyle

APRIL GLOAMING

This book is a work of fiction. Names, characters, places, and incidents are the product of the author's imagination or are used fictitiously. Any resemblance of actual events, locales, or persons, living or dead, is coincidental.

-First Edition

Publisher's Cataloguing-in-Publication Data

Doyle, Christopher K.
At the confluence / written by Christopher K Doyle
ISBN: 978-1-953932-38-9

1. Fiction – General 2. Fiction – Ghost 3. Fiction – Southern I. Title II. Author

Library of Congress Control Number: 2025943891

Praise for *At the Confluence:*

"With *At the Confluence*, Christopher K. Doyle sweeps us through landscapes Above and Below—from where the Shenandoah and Potomac Rivers meet in Harpers Ferry, to where clouds listen and candles never burn down. Built one delicately poetic sentence at a time, this shapeshifting story is a gorgeous portrait of grief and hope."

—Heather Rounds, author of *There* (Emergency Press)

"The magical objects and sleight of hand elegance of *At the Confluence* don't exist to serve their own clever ends, but to snake us along the long road back to our own humanity—and to remind us, whenever we seem in danger of forgetting, that this humanity resides in other people."

—Lily Herman, author of *Spree* (BRUISER) and *Each Day There Is a Little Love in a Book for You* (Dryad Press)

For my grandmother (Helen) and grandfather (Wendell Wesley) – the inspiration for Nora and Hollis

When there is no good or bad, no useful or useless, no up, no down, no right way,
no perfection, then okay it's not necessary that there be direction: up is down.

—Marvin Bell, *The Book of the Dead Man*

PART I:
CROSSCURRENTS

1

THERE WAS NOTHING IN THE AIR above the oak tree that Nora could see. Just a sound. A rumbling hiss like when all the water drained from the kitchen sink. Yet she couldn't stop staring. Couldn't hope to see anything else. Any color or shape. Even all the clouds from before had dispersed. As if by mutual consent. All to let her hear the last faint instant of her dear sweet husband Holly whispering above her in the wind.

Stretching out her hands, she felt for the strawberry bush—the bramble was wiry and sharp. The stickers she grasped drew the tiniest pin pricks on her fingers. She'd brought Holly's pistol with her once he'd been pulled from her (apparently, after he'd walked all the way home after drowning in the Shenandoah). Whispering in his ghostly way behind her, she'd turned to him, not understanding any of it, and watched his blue-tinged presence whisk through the kitchen window and up into the night. She'd not known a body (even a dead one) could bluster the calico drapes like that, before scattering the shattered glass at her feet.

"I just swept," was all she could muster, after she'd made the mistake of saying his name out loud, as if the dead were summoned like that. She wasn't sure what rules this world was working with, and found his pistol. The old Colt he'd kept for no other reason than he'd been given it by his uncle after their wedding night and told a man should be able to protect his family. In the drawer it sat these last eight years. But now she felt its cold weight in her apron. It sagged beneath her with a heaviness she could not fathom. Not even the hissing sound above her, or the strawberry bramble she grabbed, or the ghostly terror still racing through her— could sting her back into any semblance of what she'd been: A wife. Holly's wife. Now she just felt heavy, and knelt in the dirt, her forehead against the trunk. Trembling, her hands reached to touch the worn trigger, to feel the sad end she knew was there, waiting for her.

"Cause I'll be able to see him," she said and pointed the pistol at her pinched eye. As if through the rusty barrel Holly would be staring back, urging her on. To come with. To the other side.

"That won't work."

Nora heard the voice and looked above the oak tree, hoping Holly was still there. An eye in the dark. A presence in the highest branch, now that the clouds had returned with a rumble of thunder. "He's not there either, if you're wondering. And he wouldn't want that for you anyway."

A woman in the yard pointed at the pistol. Nora could see her shadow on a bedsheet hung from the clothesline. She was tall and shapely and seemed to float a foot above the ground—as the bedsheet billowed out in another gust—before disappearing. The kitchen lantern had sputtered out. Leaving only darkness. Without any moon to see. Without any light to show the way she thought she had to go. There was no way. Only this, and she held the pistol to her head, until she felt the lowest branches brushing her hair, calming her into this new truth: Holly was gone. The world was done; and there was nothing else to it. Turning, she slumped with her back against the tree and let the pistol sag into her lap. She'd been wrong to love him. She'd been wrong to pull further away the more the years wore on and none of their efforts had produced the child they'd wanted. *No.* She couldn't think like that. She'd been right. *They'd* been right. As right as anything she'd ever known. They'd just been distant these last years, without anyone to share their love with. When they realized Holly couldn't help her conceive. That he didn't have it in him, that ability.

"But he did have it in him." The voice sounded again, but was farther away and teased a knowledge Nora could not know. "And still does." Looking up, she watched a light approach from the house.

"How do you know what he could do?" As the light expanded and the woman came closer, Nora knew her at once and was drawn to the strange plumpness of her lips. "Miss Misery?"

"Only my customers call me Miss Misery, and you are certainly not a customer. Call me Misericordia."

"Did you see him today? Is that how you know?"

"I saw him, as I see all the dead. But he was different, your Holly. He was lost in his new state, having just drowned in that awful boat. And I daresay he must have already seen a few folks on his way home, because he was missing a few . . . parts."

Nora blinked at the word—and Miss Misery smiled to see her so curious about what she must have already known, but failed to recall after the years of disappointment.

"What I meant to say—he was magnanimous. Generous with himself. I suppose a few other folks were drawn to him as soon as he passed. Oh, I've seen it before. How someone has to say the deceased's name so they can be whisked away before any manner of strangeness occurs. The dead walking about. Looking for a way back into the rhythm of life. Into the patterns they'd crossed before. And how some living folks might ask for bits and pieces of them to fill the need they have inside themselves. To fill the emptiness. Just as easy as walking into a store and asking for pie plates or pipes."

"*Pie plates or pipes?* How about eyes?" Nora said. "I turned and he didn't have any eyes. Or heart. I tried to touch his chest, and about pushed my hand through." Nora still gaped at the image of her husband standing behind her. His blue-tinged face hushed and attentive. His hollow chest glaring at her with an emptiness she could not fathom. It didn't really seem to bother him though, and that was what confused her most.

"I'm afraid I wasn't any better. That's what I wanted to tell you."

"*How* weren't you any better?" and Nora squinted up at Misericordia.

"Well, you must've known I've not been myself these years. How I let myself go. How I didn't feel the need to keep myself presentable anymore—not that I desired anyone or anything, mind you—it was just the demands of work had me down. Of course, we haven't spoken beyond a few greetings over the years, and as you were never a customer, never needed any visions or tinctures, you couldn't know my life. And my needs."

"Why would anyone need something from the dead?"

"Everyone needs something, dear. And after today, after seeing your husband, I know there are higher needs that are sorted out, too."

"Sorted?"

"Well, meted, I suppose is the phrase. The higher needs are meted out and administered in their time."

"And that was why you saw Holly?"

"That was why he gave me something."

Nora sat up from the tree as Miss Misery leaned in, setting the candle in the grass between them. "What did he give you?"

2

HOLLY FELT THE CURRENT OF AIR AND THE CURRENT OF SONG
and the current of water moving through him—as first he expanded into the infinite
depth of existence—before contracting into the familiar shape of his body. He
reached up and his eyes were still empty sockets, his chest still gaped with a hand-
sized hole, and his lips were cracked.

Whenever he touched his lips, now that his passion had been spooled off by
that woman, he felt the rough edge against his finger. That curious woman in the
woods. *Misericordia.* Of course, he'd done business with her at the track. Buying
tinctures and medicine for the horses when he was just starting out for Mr. Marvin,
hoping to race one day for one of the stable owners—maybe even Mr. Gettys
himself. Though now he couldn't help thinking he still wanted to kiss her after
seeing her lips plump up like rose petals when they'd met on his soggy walk home.
"She'd just been waiting. On top of the ridge," he muttered, and ran his fingers along
his lips.

One moment she stood in rags and twine, covered in leaves and dirt from
rummaging about in the brush. In the next, she was kissing him. He'd stood
dumbfounded as a silver liquid like mercury hung in a long strand from his mouth.
"She'd spooled it," he recalled, and held his finger up as if he could still see it. As all
his most delicate words appeared and receded in the luminous thread. "She just
smiled as she did it, as all those rags she wore shifted into something smoother. Her
long brown bangs shook out, too, as her lips plumped up into a flowery softness,"
and another flare of wonder sparked in his mind remembering it. And in that way,
he knew she hadn't taken *all* his passion. He still felt a faint stirring to be touched.
Though there was no shame in him for thinking such thoughts, and he smiled to
know his wife had taken that remorse from him.

"Nora," he said, and saw her that last time, standing in the kitchen. She must have felt his ghostly presence behind her, because she dropped her broom and shivered when he said her name.

"He just went fishing, is all," she said. "In that damn leaky boat." Her hair was wrapped up in a bun, and as she touched the pin pulling it out, her voice echoed against the ceiling.

"*I'm sorry*," was all he could think to say. It was their wedding anniversary after all, and he hadn't brought any of the flowers she might want. Or the chocolate. Or even some of the scented candles she liked best.

"How do I know it's even you?" she finally managed, as if she could outsmart the grief welling up inside her already, denying what her heart surely knew.

"Heat," he said. "August grass. Brittle and yellow and the field alive with sound. The girls had just come up from the creek carrying sticks, while the boys were in the base paths picking sides. You wore a blue knee-length dress with white butterflies on the sleeves. There were daffodils in your hair. I'd never seen you before when your cousin introduced you. '*Visiting*,' you said. '*The whole summer*.'" He stood still. Heard the wind outside the glass. "When your cousin asked if you could play, I held my glove up as if I knew something about the places of people. About their usefulness. Ridiculous," he said, and saw a brown apple core in the dust pile at her feet. "I didn't let you play that day. I didn't let you play."

"*Holly*," she said as the memory of his shame, of not letting her play, lifted from him—even as he was pulled from her. Until all he saw were stars closing in and the oak tree stretched below, as Nora dissolved from view.

"Jesus," he muttered, remembering his last words. "Was that all I could say to her? Rambling about baseball?" and when he looked, he was back where he'd arrived, and focused on that instead. Because he still had vision, even after giving away his eyes. It seeped into his eye sockets and pores and outlined a world of sharp edges and shapes. He saw a plain of the thickest clouds. Different wind currents held shadings of pink, blue, and gold, so that the largest collection of steps he'd ever seen were outlined in airy levels. His feet shuffled out of nervousness on a stone path. There were birds above him, and tree roots dangled just out of reach. Off the roots grew the smallest silver petals that released and spun like whirligigs before reattaching to the roots. Airy harmonies from wrens and magpies swirled in a riot of sound, before realigning their songs as he took a small step forward. His clothes were still drenched from drowning and his boots squelched with each step. But the pooled water in his pockets seemed lighter here, so that he had the sensation of floating an inch above the path.

"Tribute?" A face from the clouds appeared before him. The face wore a black bowler, a scarf, and had a greasy brown mustache that drooped at the ends. It reminded him of one of the shed row gents he gambled with at the track, but he didn't know what 'tribute' meant. Patting his pockets, he searched for any coin he might offer, if indeed payment was required. "For entrance, of course. And my favor," and the man blew a perfect smoke ring even though Holly couldn't see any cigar.

"Everything went downstream when I..." Holly hesitated to say it.

"When you drowned? Come now, we're all dead here."

"Yes, when I drowned."

"There's always something. Otherwise we'd have ourselves trouble. The lines. Can you just imagine the lines?" Holly looked and there wasn't anyone behind him. There wasn't anyone in front either. *Or anything.* The stone path dissolved into a white cloud that pulsed with its own rhythm, much like how he remembered his heart, and he felt in his chest, considering it was still hard to believe he'd given it away on his walk home. Just as easy as his eyes. The man with the mustache had slumped forward throughout all this, and as Holly brought his hand back to his side, he realized he stood before a podium like at the entrance to a theater. The elbows were worn through on the man's jacket, and as he smiled, he pointed at Holly's hand. "Check again, friend."

Holding up his left hand, Holly's silver wedding band glinted between them. He'd won both bands in a craps game almost eight years ago, in 1926—and when he shook his hand and squirmed the ring free—smears of river mud reminded him of how he'd pushed against the bottom. Pushing to free himself, as the water rushed over, and his air was all but up. It had been calm, like he'd heard. A sense of brightness radiated from his fingers. Then he was on the banks completely drenched and a girl stood tugging on his hand. But he couldn't think about the girl yet, the one who needed his eyes. He saw Nora instead, on a night long before any of this. When he'd spread both rings atop a blue bedspread, and a marriage proposal had been the furthest thing on her mind. "It's silver."

"It'll do." The man placed the ring inside a vest pocket, straightened up to his full height (which wasn't very high), and raised his arm. As he did, the pulsing cloud parted into a doorway and Holly's squelching boots were moving him of their own accord. "Mind the julep now. It does pack a punch. And if you need anything—anything at all—just call. I'm Edison."

The doorway vanished as the cloud returned and Holly felt the sensation of time. Time unending. Time discarded and left to pass. He walked and the cloudy passage moved in accordance to his progress and nothing seemed to change and no amount of counting could reach a number that meant what minute or hour or month he'd spent making it to this clearing. There was a table. The edge of the step or ledge he'd followed came into focus, and as he leaned over, he couldn't see down far enough to perceive the end of light. Or above, to glimpse the edge of darkness. The next level with tree roots and birds surely remained, but all was absent of sound. That was something he just noticed—during his walk, he hadn't once uttered a word or burped in discomfort or even hummed a note in what seemed like ages. He hadn't *announced* himself in any regard. Even his squelching boots had dissolved into a great white silence, until he decided to speak to break the impasse. "Hello?"

A glass appeared on the table.

"Edison?" Stepping closer, Holly saw the mint julep. Touching the glass, he remembered the whiskey bottles in the kitchen at home, with sunrise filtering through. How in those last frustrating years he drank more and more, accumulating more bottles. Now here was mint and crushed ice and it was delicious to hear it slosh as he tilted his hand to see the bourbon catch the hazy light. Not quite evening. Not quite morning. But dusky and purple-hued. The mood had turned with him speaking. Some movement or shade of longing rippled in his mouth for the burning gulp he'd wanted in the coal mine with the boy and his drunk father. That was the man he gave his heart to. Before he'd met Misericordia on the ridge. The father had been so cruel and abusive to his son, Holly couldn't refuse. Not when he saw the need. If only the man had given him the whiskey bottle that fell from his hand after receiving the heart, Holly thought. *My heart.* And when he realized what he was wishing for, he knew the dead could still want. Wanting something burned inside him more than ever. He wanted to drink so deeply he couldn't even bring himself to taste it yet for fear of downing it in one quick jolt. *Just look*, he told himself. *Just remember.*

"You still haven't met them? You're still alone?"

Holly looked up and Edison stood beside him.

"Who's them?"

"All you have to do is drink."

3

MISS MISERY POURED THE TEA AND SWEPT THE GLASS. The broken shards had ruined Nora's clean-swept floor the instant Holly had been pulled through the window when Nora said his name. Thinking of it, Nora stared at the candle on the kitchen table. It was the one Holly had brought back with him and given to her as some sad anniversary gift. The same one Miss Misery had placed in the grass between them in the yard. The same one Nora stared at for as long as she could—her eyes hurting and her legs cramping up—until Miss Misery had plucked the pistol from her lap and mentioned something about tea and lemon peel. "With sugar," she said. "And bergamot, if you have it?" Miss Misery had already brewed the pot, after appraising the deficiency of Nora's herbs and spices. "I'll write a list," she said. "Better yet, I'll bring some of my own things that you ought to have."

Nora didn't blink but opened her mouth enough so that when Miss Misery raised the cup, Nora sipped the steaming liquid and shivered to feel the warmth move down to her belly. A bird's nest sat beside the candle, and when Nora traced the top edge—which raised a sticky dust on her finger—Miss Misery's eyes glistened.

"You wear that is what you do when you're lost, the bird's nest. I raise them in caves to keep them warm and to help them build their pretty nests. I've done so for years. They were brought over by my mother before me and by her mother as well. It's why she lived so long to begin with. Swiftlets," she said. "That's why I was up there on the ridge."

"When you saw him?" Nora didn't move. But the timbre in her voice described a lonesomeness that had Miss Misery sitting beside her, the broom still in her hand.

"When I saw him, I was checking on my darlings like always. I was worried about the last thaw, and trudged out to check. Their nests were all gone, save one. I'd been out in the brush all day by then, disconsolate and lost. You don't know. I'm the last one. I've raised these birds for as long as I can remember, and I can remember quite a lot. I placed it in my hair as I'd been taught and which my mother was taught by her mother. But I don't think any of it really mattered. I might as well have carried it in my hand. Holly smelled so deeply of love and care and passion, it was easy. The scent of it led me straight to him."

"My Holly." Pressing her hand to her belly, she ran her fingers up her neck and nose, before hesitating on her eyes, remembering the blue-tinged absence in her husband's face. He'd wavered like a shadow in that last long moment, after describing the first time they'd met, when he hadn't let her play baseball, and how ashamed he still felt. Of course, she'd forgiven him when she said his name, and then he'd been pulled into the night. Just like that. "But did he still have eyes?"

"No eyes, I'm afraid. And no heart either. And almost no passion after I was through with him, I hate to say. It was what I needed, and all I could think of these last eight years. And Holly certainly had the spark. I just spooled it on my finger. It tumbled out like thread. The idea had formed before I even knew my body was bringing me close enough to kiss him. I couldn't help but eat as much of it right there in front of him. In exchange, I gave him the bird's nest. Though I suppose someone else must have given him the candle. They must have figured he couldn't see without his eyes."

Nora's hand twitched. The fingers seemed to be looking for the pistol Miss Misery had already placed somewhere safe. Having seen this, Miss Misery pulled the pistol out from beneath a pile of napkins and placed the gun close enough for Nora's hand.

"Please listen before you decide."

"You had no right. He was dead."

"There is only what the dead and living want. It doesn't matter about right. There are needs, as I've said. They're everywhere. And the only reason I was called to him was because I had no love of my own. And haven't for years."

Nora could smell Miss Misery's minty breath and knew she didn't want to kill her. Knew she didn't want another death to be the bookend of her life, now that

Holly's passing marked a strange beginning to her somehow. There would be no more killing tonight—not for herself or this miserable woman. But she would hold the pistol to tempt the world to treat her much brighter than what all this darkness portended. And so, tipping the barrel up, she held it there as Miss Misery continued.

"The dead have come to me all my life. When I was younger, I didn't believe it. Thought it a touch of madness. An hallucination. I couldn't believe I was someone that would be demanded to see something like that. This sad procession of loss. This ceaseless passing away. The dead need to be seen by someone before they go. And after the years went on, and the shock of this endless stream of bodies became less disturbing, almost commonplace, if you can believe it, I didn't know there could be more to their visitation than my silent acknowledgment. My final affirmation of their fate. But after meeting Holly, I know there is. I've felt it."

Touching the bright plumpness of her lips, Miss Misery smoothed her hand along the length of her brown curls. Her hair ran in waves to her shoulders, and she didn't feel any twigs or leaves in it anymore. No pebbles or dirt. Even her dress—the dowdy burlap she'd grown accustomed to wearing—had changed out there in the woods. It was softer and form-fitting. The cut of which had her running her hand along her wide, shapely hips. She was desirable. Ripened. Full of the passion she'd taken from Holly, the passion swelling up inside her like a burning pulse. And placing her hand on Nora's cheek, she wanted to pass some of it on to her, but knew she couldn't. Just to give Nora a taste of what Holly had released, transferring an ounce of what she'd gotten so easily, and which she might have had more of now than she needed.

"What did it feel like? What did *he* feel like?" Nora looked at Miss Misery and saw the sudden luminescence in the woman's lips. Something silver and liquid played in the depths of them.

"Why it felt like light."

4

HOLLY TOOK A SIP OF JULEP AS EDISON WATCHED. Though before the bourbon could go down, before the ice cubes even clinked, Edison was gone and the table had transformed into a barroom. On a bandstand, a bass player, guitarist, and clarinetist spun through a swinging jazz number. Stunned, Holly moved toward a poker game where several rough characters laughed and smoked cigars as waitresses in short black skirts buzzed between the tables. Customers spilled across the room. They tapped their feet and talked in a confusion of voices as the bartender poured drinks and even winked at Holly—who stood on the outside of it all—as if on the outside of a snow globe looking in. The mint julep had vanished from his hand.

"You shouldn't have given it to him." A man at the table touched his wide fedora and scowled at Holly.

"You screwed up, is what he's saying." Another man stood in a huff and leaned toward Holly but only came up to his armpit. Another man had to grab the little man's arm to settle him down. He called him McCallan before pulling him back.

"I died is what happened," Holly said.

"No shit. We're all dead, but at least we knew enough to die the right way."

"And not give anything up."

"At least not yet."

Holly shuddered to hear the voices call at him in a conversation beyond his knowing. He'd died, of course, and all of them were dead. And, yes, he'd given things away—his eyes and heart and passion. But he hadn't any choice. There were rules he didn't know anything about. Whenever they flashed like newspaper print in his mind, he had to follow them. First off, there'd been the girl on the riverbank after he drowned. She'd tugged on his hand and asked for his eyes, considering her grandmother was almost blind and afraid to look at the death coming so soon for her. So, he obliged. As easy as pulling stones from the mud. Then the boy near the coal mine with the awful father, the man who needed his heart. So, he handed it over. Then Misericordia in the woods—without any passion or love of her own—and of course, he couldn't refuse anything they needed, and that was all he knew to say. "I couldn't refuse. It's a rule."

"Holy shit. You're gonna come in here with your dumb face and head without a hat and tell *me* what you can't refuse? *Me?* The one who knows the rules and helped write them up and who still administers them to this day?"

"Bigs, Bigs." The little man McCallan moved to hold Bigs back. A waitress hovered close by and handed Bigs a shot, which he slugged, before licking his lips and glaring at Holly.

"Edison probably didn't tell him," she said and touched Bigs's arm before looking at Holly with a sad smile. "He's just ignorant, is all. All the way through. You don't see too many like that anymore. All waterlogged and squelchy in their boots. Probably didn't even hear the current calling to him when it happened either."

"No, no," Holly said. "I didn't hear anything. Honest." Holly was hot. Sweat lined his brow. His boots squeaked as he swayed back and forth, while his jacket dripped a growing puddle beneath him. "I heard water is all. Then the girl asked me where my boat was. That was before the three policemen laughed out on the rapids, after dislodging my boot."

"Jesus. Just ignorant." Clucking her tongue, the waitress was off as Bigs straightened his tie and unrolled his sleeves. He'd reclaimed a sense of ease in hearing Holly's misunderstanding of the whole situation.

"But that doesn't mean you give anything away. Just like that. Do you see this?" and Bigs chuckled to know Holly's eyes were just creased pits in his face. "I gave this out only after I knew." Dislodging his left eye, he held it up for Holly to see. "It's a replacement, is what I'm saying. Something I earned *after* I traded for it." Twisting off his left hand, Bigs shook the fingers that held the eye so Holly could see the parts they all had in them to give. Unscrewing both thumbs, McCallan juggled them as he smiled. Another man placed an ear on the table. Another, his nose. All the parts and pieces symbolizing the work Holly knew he now had to complete in becoming whole again.

"You've been called up here without knowing," McCallan said. "Hell, you didn't even hear the calling crying out to you."

"What was it—the song above the oak tree before the storm?" Bigs shook his head and eased back the brim of his hat to think of Holly's circumstances. "It was calling just for you, dumb dumb. The same way it does for everyone," and plopping his eye back in and reattaching his hand, he looked at Holly a long time.

"There was only Nora. That was all I could see," Holly said. "She said my name and then the wind pulled me up into a darkness folding over into stars."

"Jesus." Bigs stepped back to appraise the man standing there without any eyes or heart or passion. "But you're here, ain't you? After all that. You're here and you give me the creeps, water boy. It's all out of order is what it is."

"It's unnatural," McCallan chimed in.

"Impertinent," someone from the table added.

"It's just a mistake. A big mistake." Holly stepped toward Bigs, imploring him, begging him to understand. "I didn't know any of it. That I'd have to know anything or do things in order to die correctly? Doesn't that count for something? *For anything?* Now all I do is what the rules say before I can even stop to think."

"Oh, I'll give you time to think, water boy. All the time you could ever hope where you're headed."

5

MISS MISERY WARMED THE BIRD'S NEST in a pot on the stove. Just as she'd done for years on her own, remembering how her mother had cooked the nests when customers paid all they could to have a bowl of the syrupy concoction. They came from all over the hills once they heard. News spread fast amongst the old timers and invalids. The bird's nest soup (mixed with wild berry and rock sugar) could ease the arthritis and dispel the dyspeptic. Added zing to the heartstrings, and clarity of mind to a cobwebbed head. Miss Misery remembered her mother's roll call of all the ailments the bird's nest soup relieved. As if there'd never been a medicine or tincture to rival the steaming, bubbling salve she stirred beneath her. Inhaling its essence was like being home. She looked up and Nora had vanished, but returned with a blanket wrapped around her shoulders. Holly's candle still burned before her and shined on the other object she hadn't brought herself to decipher. Why had a dead man dropped a metal clasp to the floor in his last moment? Nora looked at the clasp and pondered. *Who'd given it to him?* She wore no belt loop to clip it to, no chain or strap, and nudged it with her finger. Turning it over, she saw how it glinted in the candlelight and imagined the silver spark in Miss Misery's lips when she'd kissed him.

It had been completely unexpected. Of that, Nora was certain. Miss Misery couldn't have anticipated such a thing. Or Holly. But Nora imagined how an electric hum must have escaped when their mouths touched. Because she could still picture Miss Misery leaning in, as the heat rose from her flesh, and all the hair stood up on her arms. When there was still an inch between them, Miss Misery would have closed her eyes, but still seen the silver light stretched between them on the backdrop of her mind. Then all would have been a soft warmth. Miss Misery would have felt a spark spreading until it felt like bright flames might stand off the ends of her fingers. Like off the candlewick Nora so desperately watched. Was Holly inside the light? Was that what Miss Misery meant when she said it felt like light, the passion she'd spooled off of him? She wanted to know. *Needed* to know, until even when she shut her eyes the light pulsed in the center of her vision.

"Here." Miss Misery stood above Nora with a steaming bowl and a few pieces of toast. "It'll help you see things," and setting down the pistol, Nora pushed it away.

"What's there to see beyond this light? He came all the way back from the dead to give it to me."

"And the clasp," Miss Misery reminded her.

"And the clasp—of which I have no earthly idea the use."

"And this soup." Miss Misery nudged Nora's elbow, and as the first spoonful went down, Nora was quiet. Not tired or withdrawn. But reflective. Miss Misery watched as the candlelight seemed to find a hollow in Nora's cheeks upon which to rest. Rose and gold shades bathed her skin as the shadows drew back. The light was all-consuming and true. Enveloping.

"She was going to be just like me," Nora said, before tasting another mouthful. "She'd have long auburn curls and green eyes and freckles along the ridge of her nose. In the morning, she'd run downstairs in her pajamas right out into the yard to the strawberry bush. Each sunrise she'd pick a handful and eat them right there in the rising warmth. Smeared strawberry juice on the corners of her mouth and on the sides of her hands. Ellie or Elise or Emmie. *Evangeline?* I was never sure. But wanted a girl with an E to start her name. Always did like that sound. Holly never could decide."

Recognizing the moment, as Miss Misery often had, having trained herself with her customers, she knew a fantasy when she heard one. Knew the hushed tones of a voice filled with sorrow. Knew the girl in the vision had never come to pass. Had only ever been dreamed of and spoken about with a rapture bordering on a mania. And here it was. Spilled out by the balm of the bird's nest. And all she could do was listen—to the life Nora detailed in such fine notes of sadness—Miss Misery couldn't help but see the little girl standing before them.

"She always had cuts on her cheeks. Small little sticker bush cuts because of the fort she built with Holly out beyond the oak. They wore capes I made from old bed sheets I hadn't seen fit to donate to the Ruritan. She said they were pirates or marauders and whenever I set an apple pie or cinnamon rolls out to cool, I always expected at least one missing bite before I brought them in. I never mentioned it though. Thought it a small price to pay for the enjoyment I got hearing them rambling out beyond the light, out past the flower bed and wheelbarrow. Out past everything that made her so much a part of everything here." Nora turned from the empty whiskey bottles above the doorway; they'd just caught the first sunlight. It had been night already, and Miss Misery hadn't once mentioned sleep. Knew sleep wasn't where Nora needed to be. Not with so many feelings still pulling her up into the tempest of her sadness. This current was memory, and Nora needed to ride it as long as it pulsed in the air above them, as long as it sustained her.

"I only made her seven. That was all I got to. What *we* got to. I figured one year after we married, then it begins. The baby and toddler years were frantic. I felt her growing, learning things, seeing animals and drawing shapes and pictures. Words came quickly with her. *She just has a way*, was all I could think to tell folks in town and friends who visited. A natural affinity. She loved anything to do with music and singing. By the seventh year, she was already writing her own stories and sending letters to faraway kingdoms. There was always a party or ball she had to attend, and we spent many nights measuring and sewing the last hem to make sure it all fit. Her gown. Her slippers. Her crown."

"Seven is just fine, dear."

"Seven was all I could do," and Nora's chest heaved a long breath as if the effort of remembering was too much for her anymore.

Miss Misery had her arm around Nora's shoulder. The soup was done. Nora had scraped the last spoonful and held the clasp in her hand. She needed to move. Needed to take the candle with her wherever her legs might decide, and Miss Misery could sense it. Could sense the man beyond the gate before she even let Nora go. Could see the shiny badge. Feel the nervousness in him. The dread.

Considering he'd been the one who'd shook Holly's boot free from in-between the slick river rocks. Out where the water pressed down. Surging with such force. Miss Misery could still feel Holly's hands against the murky bottom, pushing with all his might—pushing until he looked and a radiant substance not unlike milk drifted from his fingers.

"*Mame?* Mrs. Hollis Pride?" A knocking brought Nora up from the table and down from fantasy's current. Another current held her now. One coursing through the kitchen, moving her to the front door. She'd put the candle in a wooden holder, with a carved saucer to catch the dripping wax, which never seemed to drip from the small, steady light. It was curious. Even when Nora shook it to readjust the clasp in her other hand, the light was always steady.

"I'm Officer Wray," he said and held his hat in his hand. Nora hadn't opened the screen door. Just stood in the candlelight and watched it instead. Didn't need to see his face. Didn't need to read his downturned eyes to know what she'd felt as soon as Holly had appeared behind her last night whispering her name. "There's been an accident."

"Don't you think I know that?" Nora said, and slamming the screen door, she was already moving. He wanted her to identify the body at the station, but she couldn't. The current had pushed her off, unmoored her, and Miss Misery knew she couldn't follow. Not yet. But that all things and people would eventually return here. To this house. To this oak tree and hill. Once the currents met up again.

PART II: SHADOWS AND LIGHT

6

"DEATH, MUCH LIKE LIFE, IS ALL A MATTER OF TIMING." Holly heard Clevenger's voice before he saw him. Just as he had these last few days. Though there really weren't any days anymore. Or hours. Or any distinction of night. Even if Holly needed to think there still was. Even if he needed to see time as a tool for organizing the way things went. As if winding some perpetual clock meant that Nora would still be a central force in his life. Someone with a routine of waking and breathing and sleeping. So he imagined time moving above him in airy currents with a specific destination. Something that spoke of a movement forward. Instead of this dry dusty stasis—this entire lack of movement even though all these days he'd been walking, walking.

Holly looked up, and the air held a hovering gray mist. It pervaded the crumbling trail he trudged on—a dry riverbed or gulley—drained of the color and water it once held. He'd turn his head and Clevenger would be there on his mule Callous. That was the beast's name, and a more fitting moniker Holly couldn't conceive. The animal was mean. Had spat and bared his brown cracked teeth whenever Holly had first touched his shaggy hide. Holly had learned never to venture forth so close again.

"What do you see?" Holly spoke and Clevenger appeared above the gulley riding Callous. Holly had wondered at the binoculars slung from Clevenger's neck from the first moment he'd appeared here. It happened so suddenly. He'd been standing before Bigs in the barroom. He'd been begging and pleading with Bigs that it was all a mistake. That he didn't know. He hadn't heard the current calling to him and what it instructed. Then here he was. As far down as he could go. At least, as far down as Clevenger knew there was to go.

"Nothing." Clevenger paused with Callous to look off ahead. The gulley rose so slightly, it was hard to tell they were climbing with each step. But Holly felt it in his legs.

23

Every movement was a fraction more draining than the last. Though he never seemed drained completely of the steps he had to take. His body was in charge here, and had been for longer than he realized. Even in the other world. When he'd been alive.

"At the track," he muttered, and Clevenger lowered the binoculars to hear Holly speak.

"You're talking about your life again; I just know it. I can smell it. It smells like—apple pie—and saddle oil. That's your life. All of us have smells inside. Smells that sum up what we've lost and want to keep true."

"Smells?"

"Of course. You don't think you smell something you love, and it dissolves? Why would our bodies ever be made that way?"

Holly hadn't considered all the smells his nose had taken in. The rosy and putrid scents that it both coveted and pushed aside. Much like all the images his eyes had seen (if he still had eyes to flutter and roll and blink), and he could sense his eye sockets clenching tighter to feel the gray mist invade their emptiness. All those older images were there, he was sure, in his sockets. Or his mind. So why not the smells?

"Is that why saddle oil is one of yours? I have a very good sense about these things. I smelled you right away."

"I gambled. A bit too much, I'm afraid. It was only during the down times. Which was probably why it made things worse. I'd lose a job hauling flour sacks or replacing someone's shingles, and instead of saving all I'd made, I'd try to double or triple it at the track."

"No wonder Callous hates you. He could smell horses as soon as you arrived." Callous nodded in agreement and bared his brown cracked teeth just to make sure Holly still knew. "He doesn't like horses."

"Well, there were definitely horses. Some mornings I'd ride for trainers when a jockey couldn't make it. I was never good enough to race though. A bit too tall. Always stood up too high in the saddle. Always felt like I might need to jump off, they ran so fast. So I guess it was just my body back then taking over, too. When it knew my strength and confidence weren't enough."

"None of us are ever enough, Holly. It's not just you." Clevenger had slipped his binoculars off and held them out for Holly, as was their routine. Clevenger would look ahead while Holly looked behind, so that both felt like they were in charge of some direction.

"Nora didn't know, of course, the way I bragged and carried on." Holding the binoculars, Holly turned to look back. Far off, there was a commotion of dust. Like a twirling cone of sand and soil. Something he'd see now and then when he thought there might be someone following. But it was nothing. A stir of wind. A trick of light. "And some days I'd get an inside tip and make enough to pretend it'd be alright, me not working just then. But most days, I wouldn't."

"Anything?"

"Nothing." Holly handed the binoculars back. His arms were still drenched, just like his pants. And it was one of the things he didn't mind so much. Sticking out his tongue, a few drops of river water fell from his nose, and he could still taste what living was like. Could still taste the rushing current that drowned him. And by doing so—that traumatic moment—gave him memory. And comfort, as odd as that sounded. The comfort of who he was and what life was like with the river rushing over, and the sunlight fading fast, and the windowsill steaming with a fresh baked apple pie. All as he strolled home with another empty whiskey bottle to place above the door.

"The dead go back to where they die. At least, the troubled dead do."

Holly was used to Clevenger's strange pronouncements and tried to memorize them. Much like the rules he'd still see once a rule was ready to be seen. The man saw inside Holly like he'd never felt, except maybe with Nora. As if all his thoughts were nothing more than pages Clevenger thumbed through whenever the silence of the gulley and the long looks through the binoculars returned nothing again and again.

"Aren't we all troubled being dead?

"More and less."

"Don't you mean more or less?"

"Of course not. I meant more *and* less. There are more-troubled dead and less-troubled dead. And you are most certainly more troubled. With Nora. And what she wanted."

"And what did she want?" Holly shivered to ask, because Nora was here in their words, and how he thought of her. Of course, he'd always known what she wanted: *A child*. One with an E starting her name. With freckles and strawberry hair and green piercing eyes. The one Nora always summoned up in the quiet moments of their love. The one he'd never been able to give her, but now hoped to find somehow—this girl—this miraculous manifestation. The one he had to locate or fabricate from circumstance, from somewhere out there, on the other end of the binoculars. The one that might give some meaning to all this, and some hope. The one he imagined might save him.

7

"AIN'T NOTHING DOWN THERE BITING this morning, mame." A man coming up from the river had seen Nora's candle and walked straight toward it. She'd been out a few hours by then, not knowing where the candle would lead. But she trusted her legs. Believed in them even after the first raindrops had started and then ceased, but which left her hair wet and her dress clinging to her back and thighs. Shuffling from foot to foot to warm herself, she heard the metal clasp rattling in her apron. Looking down, she realized she still wore her apron. The blanket she'd started out with had gotten caught on a branch not fifteen minutes from home, and in her state (with an overwhelming desire to move), she'd left it there because she felt time racing ahead. Felt that there was never enough time to remember Holly and to recover the bits and pieces of his life. What was his smile like in the morning? And his smell? She felt whiskey was one, certainly. On his hair and breath. Something hot and sweet steaming up. And horses. She still smelled horses.

"Just some smallmouth bass, but not worth the worms to bait 'em."

Nora blinked as he walked past her smiling, before stopping not ten paces off to look back at the light.

"Sure is something," he said, and shook his fishing rod at the candle. "Kind of reminds me of."

Nora waited to hear him complete the thought that had been important enough to stop him in his tracks. But there was nothing. The man just smiled and took the canvas fishing hat from his head. He waved it once near his ear to shoo away a black fly and then bowed to her abruptly.

Nora had seen nothing like it. She'd never understood the ways of men. Their habits. And rigid absurdity. But after watching him long enough and considering him harmless, she started off again atop her legs. Her legs, her legs. Medium-length and sturdy and with the slightest pinch in the left knee, but which the hours of walking had helped work out. Now there were no arms or limbs beneath her anymore. She held the candle, but did not feel her hand. She stepped over roots and stones, but could not feel her tattered house slippers. Or even hear the flip-flopping sound they made smacking the dirt-packed trail that stretched out like an unspooled thread. Something meandering and errant strung beneath the trees. She looked back every so often, and sure enough the man still followed her at a respectful distance. Maybe twenty paces now. His fishing rod jangling above him and his floppy hat still in his hand.

"I ain't going fishing," she said (though she wasn't sure what her body might decide). Thinking this might be enough to dissuade him from following her, she could hear the river now that it was close. It roared somewhere on the other side of the trees. A rushing, vacuous taking away was what it sounded like. Something that had stolen her Holly with its appetite. A yawning, gaping jaw with a thirst that thousands and millions of perpetual gallons couldn't sate, so that it even needed to swallow Holly down. "*The bitch*," she said and clenched her fist around the clasp, thinking of the bitchy river. The monstrous length of it. Accepting everything given to it by rocks and valley and sky, and always moving on and devouring anything else that came in contact with it. "The whore."

"Excuse me?"

The man must have heard her and been confused, but when she looked, there was another person with him. An older woman in a gray sweater with an apple basket stood looking at her. Or more accurately, the candle. The light never wavered and was small, but gave off a constant glow that Nora didn't even register after staring at it all night. She just knew its constancy would never waver. Holly had left it for her. He'd trudged back across a divide of life and death to place it rolling at her feet. So with the bird's nest in her belly, and the clasp in her fist, she kept the candle—always the candle—out ahead.

"Is that the," the woman said, but she didn't say any more.

"Of course it's the." The man hadn't turned, but just confirmed what he and the woman must have known inside to be true. What some need compelled them to see.

Nora didn't know the woman. Or the man. She only saw them as symptoms of Holly's death now. Some lingering strands from the nether world come to haunt the living a while longer. Something announced by their presence, but never deciphered. Not all the way. But maybe something her body could take care of, because it was already moving. It ducked her beneath a branch, jumped her over a puddle, and then stepped her out atop the banks. The rapids bubbled and popped as sunlight shimmered across the whole moving surface. Holly had died somewhere down there. He'd been stolen by those swift turning waters. Thinking of it, she spat into the rapids and watched that small floating bit of her drift for the longest second before being dragged down to the depths.

"Well, I heard about the."

"Is this where the."

"I thought I saw a."

"Ain't it just like them to bring a."

Another and another person had arrived. She could feel them staring at the candle. At the light that was hers. And right then she had it in her mind to blow it out. To let the compulsion they must have felt in seeing it, or hearing its soft wavering voice—calling to them in the darkest caverns of their wanting and longing—to be snuffed out. So that it was her alone that got to see the small burning essence of his love. Because that was what it was, she knew. His love. Holly had returned it to remind her it was always there with her. It had to be.

"Well, I just knew I had to."

"Mothers and saints in all the."

"I just couldn't believe it when I first."

Her body stepped quicker along the banks as she followed the candle, which followed the Shenandoah. The rumble of feet behind her at times canceled out the river sounds when they passed a placid stretch where the rapids didn't run, and it was just a languid pulse. With the sun higher, she could see Harpers Ferry on the other side. Its church spires and cobbled streets etched into the Blue Ridge. She hadn't known so many lived so close to the water here. But more came out and said their half-completed thoughts, then got in line as they moved as some human river all their own behind her—and still the candle blazed on. Still not an inch of tallow had burned down in all the hours since Miss Misery had lit it, and Nora wiped sweat from her brow for the day had grown steamy. A breeze blustered the treetops as the roaring sound of the river returned. They'd reached the Shenandoah Staircase (for that was what they called it around here). It stretched out almost half a mile. Big boulders shaped like steps burst through the water. Enough to batter and wreck the sturdiest craft. And life. Holly's life.

"Miss? I'm not sure that's wise."

Nora wasn't sure she'd heard it right. Someone had been able to complete a full sentence? She turned and almost fifteen people stood there. They'd reached a small bit of sandy shore. But when she heard the voice again, not one of the people behind her had spoken, and she thought a spirit from the river was casting out its warning.

"Miss, I'm up here."

"Oh, Holly." Raising her head, she expected to see the dark outline of her love—but the navy-blue uniform of an officer materialized. Nora had walked so far along the river, she'd brought her devoted gathering close enough to the two-lane road cut higher up in the ridge. Cars swooshed by at the edge of hearing on their way to the racetrack in Charles Town, almost eight miles west.

"I'm just going where I have to," she said.

"Is that so?" He stood in-between Nora and the crowd, and right away her body could tell there was no deeper need in him. He couldn't see or feel whatever the others did in the candle, and had certainly been one of them—one of the officers who'd pulled Holly up by his boot. There'd been three of them, her mind told her. This was the second. The first had come to her door to tell her Holly was gone. But this one was taller. More confident and colder. His hand held some blurry register of touch. She looked and his right hand shifted into a watery current, until she had to squint to recover the hard shape of his fingers. "I want y'all to get," he said. Turning, he shooed them with his big hands, but the crowd didn't budge. In fact, they seemed more than willing to stampede him for keeping them from seeing as clearly as they wanted the candle, which burned steady through it all. "Did you hear? Get. Go on now. *Get.*"

Nora watched stone-faced as the crowd sadly pulled back into the shadows and craggy hollers. Back to the faint footpaths and trails that would take them home. She didn't like the officer, but appreciated the authority to dispel the whole lot of them. To leave her to the whims of her body. She wasn't sure where it would take her, but she could feel the depths inside her, and the end to which Holly'd been pulled. How his long strong arms had stretched out to touch the murky bottom. To push himself free. When his air was all but up, and the water was crashing down. She knew she needed to stay here for as long as her body demanded it. As long as these feelings of Holly remained like an echo inside her. Even after the policeman trudged off. Even after his car door slammed shut and the tires swooshed away. Then it was just the candle, the metal clasp, the bird's nest in her belly, and a small girl emerging from behind a tall fern. Her strawberry hair shimmered in the sharp piercing light reflecting off the water.

8

THE SLIGHTEST PULSE OF LIGHT LIFTED the grayness enough so that Holly could see his own shadow. It wasn't stretched out very far, but had crafted a circle beneath each step as he moved along the gulley. He hadn't seen Clevenger in a few hours, but could still sense his presence, and wondered if Clevenger could see him in these moments? If whatever force or rule that prevailed here kept them separate in the silence, but then together in the speaking? What were the rules and who made them?

"What's happening here?" Clevenger appeared and cantered on Callous on the gulley rim. "You have a shadow?"

"I have a shadow." Holly grinned and flapped his arm to see the corresponding shadow in the dirt.

"But that's . . . not possible? Where's this light coming from?"

"I looked and it just seemed to be growing as I looked, and then I wondered if it was something you might have seen before or known about?" Holly giggled to stretch out both arms and see his shadow flapping like a bird. He then tried to remember the last time he'd laughed?

For a moment, Holly thought Clevenger might dismount Callous to inspect the shadow beneath them on the rim. But at a cluck of his tongue, the wide beast paused and began to lean forward ever so slightly, so that Clevenger could inspect this new phenomenon closer. Holly had not seen Clevenger lean so much as an inch from Callous, and the sight of his friend like this had him smiling to think that maybe in the hundreds of years that Clevenger had been here, the air had never brightened like this. Or pulsed as it did now. To feel the utter elation at something as minute as this wash over them, had Holly stepping closer to see how Clevenger reacted.

"Why, it's the damndest thing I've ever seen. I can see my shadowy head and Callous, his broad shoulders, his clenched muzzle?" Clevenger looked wide-eyed before pulling a handkerchief from his pocket to wipe his brow. Callous had turned slightly at this unusual movement, and for an instant, Holly had seen the other side of the animal—and it occurred to him he'd never seen the other side of the animal before. Clevenger and Callous always kept a right profile to Holly's inspection. But now that the mule had turned enough, Holly could see his distended torso. Bulges of fatty shapes stretched out from the animal's other side. From his thigh and rump, his side and chest, it looked as if a whole other animal was submerged in his depths, and Holly shuddered to see the gelatinous shapes quiver as Clevenger finally leaned back and their regular profile returned.

"And you started seeing this change when?" Clevenger wiped his face again, held the binoculars to his eyes, and looked almost directly up for the origin of this stunning change.

"Just a few hours ago I noticed my hand. I mean, I looked, and it didn't seem as blurry as before, as dim. Then I looked to the side and noticed a shadow of my hand stretched below. Just like that. Then it grew a bit more, as if the light intensified. And then it stopped and remained steady. It's the same steady light you see now."

"Remarkable. I'd say it's the most remarkable thing I've seen since I've been here. And I've been here longer than I can remember."

"Is there some rule about this that you know?"

"Let me think. We are in the Below. You came from the Above for the Drowned Dead. I thought I told you all this."

"No, we never really..."

"There are many different deaths, of course, and many different degrees of dying. There is an Above for all of them. They tend to gather like with like, taking stock of what they have before moving them on."

"They?"

"Well, certainly. You wouldn't want to gather two unlike deaths and try to deal with them similarly. It'd be a disaster. Might rend the realm in two or something. You met Mr. Bigs, of course?"

"Unfortunately."

"He's a rather nasty sort, I'll admit. Doesn't like things out of order in the least. And I'm afraid all that power's gone to his head. But he's been in charge of sorting the more-troubled drowned dead since before I was here, so…"

"Jesus, that's even a category—the more-troubled drowned dead?"

"Sometimes it feels like there are more categories than people. More-troubled drowned dead, less-troubled drowned dead, slightly-abused drowned child, miscellaneous and farmstead drownings, water well drownings, drainage ditch drownings. Etcetera. Etcetera."

"And you were going to tell me all this—when?"

"I was hoping we'd run into someone. Sort of in a hands-on type training. Where we could really drive home the learning. Then you could possibly exchange something for the body parts you've lost. I'm afraid you really can't move on unless you're as complete as when you started. The dead cannot continue apart. You must be together. Whole."

Holly felt the absence in his chest as soon as Clevenger said it. His hand had become accustomed to the deep gaping absence, knew the sharp edge of each snapped rib. Smoothing over the velvety rise and fall of his lungs, he could still see the boy in the coal mine smiling to feel the beating heart in his hand. The heart Holly had given him, before plunging it into his father's chest. He remembered what he'd felt in that instant—when his heart went in to right the wrongs of that ruined man—he'd felt like a father. He'd felt what it meant to open yourself to the pains and struggles of the world, the fear and irrational optimism that came with pushing your child out to live a life you couldn't control. A life beyond your knowing. It was a helpless, falling feeling, but it was suffused with hope and love. A love bigger than he'd ever felt before. And it was this love he wanted to tell Nora about. To touch her. To hold her shoulders and speak. Telling her what having a child was like, so that maybe she could imagine the life they'd never been able to share. But when he'd seen her, he could only utter her beautiful name and remind her of when he didn't let her play baseball.

"*Why* you must be whole is another matter altogether," Clevenger said as Callous started off again. They trotted now as Clevenger leaned over at intervals to see the shadow following each step. "The soul can't change, can it?"

"It can't?"

"Of course not, so we rarely discuss it. Judgements are made on character and choices, obviously. And who does the deciding and choosing?"

Holly blinked at Clevenger and stumbled in the gulley following him. As his wet boots scrunched the dry earth, each step sent up little clouds of dust that swirled in a brief vortex before dispersing. And it occurred to him he might not have been able to answer Clevenger's question in another hundred years of walking.

"Why the body, of course," and Clevenger stopped Callous to look down at Holly. "The body does the deciding and choosing and living and dying. So, it's of course important for the body to be returned whole after living. No matter what death. No matter what manner of disfigurement or trauma. The dead are required to return the body as whole as when they got it. That, my friend, is most definitely a rule."

"Well, how do I do that here?"

"It's obvious—we find someone."

9

NORA SAT UPON THE BANKS FOR MANY HOURS THAT DAY. She sat in silence and watched the candlelight pulse and the daylight pass through, and still the girl sat beside her, wordless and attentive. Whenever Nora stood to stretch her legs, the girl stood and stretched her legs, too. Even though she was so young and spry, she wouldn't have needed to stretch anything to stay seated like that for as long as it took.

"As long as it takes," Nora muttered, and the girl smiled. "Is that what you decided?"

"Mame?"

"That you'd sit here for as long as it takes to see whatever it is the candle shows people. Is that what all the others want, too?"

"I think all the others want other things."

"And how do you know that?"

"Just a feeling. I've gotten all these feelings lately. Like there's another voice in there all a sudden." The girl touched her belly as if to show Nora where she meant this other voice resided. It was getting colder with the night coming on, but Nora and the girl didn't seem to mind. From the candle they not only found a focus for their needs—in Nora, to reconnect with Holly in any way she could, following her body wherever it went—and the girl. Though Nora wasn't quite sure what the girl's needs were.

"I'm Nora," she said. Names hadn't been necessary in the long stillness of their vigil. They'd existed as twin sensibilities. As if the girl, in her silent companionship, was a living shadow of Nora's steady watchfulness.

"Juniper." The girl didn't raise her hand in greeting or move at all. She didn't even make eye contact, and Nora felt herself deficient in the few moments she'd turned from the candle to stare at the girl for this new show of friendship. "Most call me Juney though. Live right up in the holler." She pointed back and up, and Nora couldn't see the ridge anymore. Its dark shape rose above them and then dissolved, merging with the night. Only the water rushing past was of any concern. The twinkling lights of Harpers Ferry hovered on the other side. Occasionally, they heard snatches of fiddle and guitar carrying over the water. Someone was dancing somewhere. Someone was having fun.

"That's a nice name. It sounds . . . *fresh*." Nora smiled and it was the first time she'd smiled in days. She hadn't remembered what it was like to feel happy. Holly's death had drained all that. But it was nice now on the riverside in the dark. It was nice to talk with Juney. To sit and think.

"It's okay as far as names go, I guess. I've never been teased if that's what you mean. Some people call me Juney Bug though, because of the song."

Nora blinked at the girl and for the life of her couldn't recall ever hearing any song with a Juney Bug in it.

"From 'Froggy Went A'Courtin'. The Juney Bug was the first to come in. Way down yonder in a hollow log?" Nora stared vacantly at Juney's words. "The wedding between Froggy and Miss Mousey," Juney replied. "She brought in the water jug." Juney looked at Nora, who shrugged her shoulders at Juney Bug with a water jug. "Ain't you ever sung to your kids before?"

Nora's hand quivered at mention of her kids. There was only one she'd ever imagined. But what would *children* be like? And how many could she have? Dozens didn't seem right. And one was all she'd ever let herself believe was possible. But that was before they realized Holly couldn't even help with one. Though Miss Misery did say he had it in him. But did he have it in him for three? Because three sounded right. Three was a number to believe in and hold fast. Definitely three. "No, I never had any children."

"Oh." Juney hadn't known anyone who didn't know about Froggy and Miss Mousey, and she almost had it in her mind to sing the whole song right there, but it was a long one, and she was more in a staring and wondering mood than a singing mood. Since she'd first seen the woman holding it, the candle looked awful familiar to her. Juney had just left the sheriff's office. She'd walked most of the morning to tell the sheriff her grandmother had passed the night before. The coffin that had already been ordered and paid for had been delivered to her grandmother's specifications. She just needed someone to help move her into it. They had a family plot in the cemetery in Harpers Ferry. Way up the hill on the other side of the Shenandoah, and Juney would need the sheriff to transport the coffin for her, too (she had no other family). She'd spoken with him not fifteen minutes before she'd seen the candle. Or rather—heard it. It was strange. How to describe a sound from light? Kind of like a song really. A straggle of notes and strings. Something shaped more like the struggle of a bird rising to fly before drifting calm and steady in an updraft. Something unseen and heated that kept the bird aloft for hours as all the world passed below, oblivious to the invisible threads supporting everything and everyone.

"The song is faint now. But it's there," Juney said and stared at the candle, and she knew right then where she'd seen it—because it was hers. Or rather, it was the candle she'd given the dead man to help him on his way, so he could see.

"The Froggy song?" Nora asked.

"No, the other song," and Juney pointed at the candle and touched her ear, even though she didn't bend or move an inch to get closer to it.

"Is that what you need? Is that what you want from it?" Nora nodded at the candle and held it closer, so it might be that much easier for Juney to hear whatever it was she heard. Though even then, echoes of oars sounded far off on the Potomac. The bright noise rose below Harpers Ferry, where the two rivers met. And Nora wondered why one river got to take over the other in the first place. Why did one current get to be stronger? And who decided?

"It's not something I can describe," Juney said. "It's just there," and she pointed at the candle and then her chest, and it refocused Nora's attention. "It started last night, if you must know. Right before Grandma passed. After the dead man gave her his eyes."

His eyes. Nora couldn't breathe, and saw the emptiness in his face. Saw his beautiful blue eyes gone and the sockets staring at her, imploring her somehow even without any color or living spark. She bent closer to ask Juney what she meant, when the first rowboat appeared. It came careening toward the candle and slammed to a jutting stop; two boys and a woman sat staring from the bow. "I just knew it was."

"Just like they all said, and I'll just bet."

"No, I never did believe you until we were."

Other voices were rising in the darkness and moving closer. Nora looked at the woods on the edge of the banks and faces appeared. Bodies walked out in a mass of dirty overalls and mud-smeared boots. They'd been waiting all this time. Hiding behind trees and brush after the officer had scared them off. But the officer hadn't put out the candle. He hadn't once come near enough or needed it as far as Nora could tell. And when three more boats came thudding through the river, Nora looked up to see a silent and attentive crowd gathered before her like before a preacher in a church, and she had no earthly idea what her body might do?

10

THE SWIRLING SHAPE DANCED AND SWAYED BEHIND THEM. Though in another instant it dispersed as soon as Holly had run the one hundred yards or so to see if it was someone who'd appeared. Just as he'd checked those other times before. Another body come to trade parts with—if indeed the person needed to trade anything at all.

"There!" Holly yelled and was off again as another vortex appeared. He ran and his boots squelched and the binoculars swung from his neck as he huffed his way as fast as he could to meet the person—if indeed it was a person—but it wasn't. Just another shape of dust. A whispered breeze. A dry, brittle disappointment.

"Please?" Clevenger said, and held his hand out for the binoculars. Clevenger was still enthralled with the light that brought the grayness around them to a lighter shade. He looked up for a long moment, then lowered the binoculars, then held his hand out, turning it over to see the shadow mirroring his life. "You know, it's not really supposed to change here. At least, I've never seen it change before. Not in all my time."

"Why wouldn't it change?" Holly kicked a pebble, and it rolled downhill, before resting on a pile of rubble. He still scoured the gulley behind them. But as far as he could tell, there was nothing. Not even another vortex of dust and debris. He'd spotted twelve whirlwinds over the last few days and had run up on each of them, only to be disappointed again and again.

"I don't think it's supposed to," Clevenger continued. "It's not that kind of place."

"And what kind of place is it?"

Patting Callous, Clevenger rubbed his hand along the mule's neck. Callous had reared up at Holly's question. He'd even bared his teeth, and Holly thought the mule might spit at him, or rush down from the rim to take out whatever hatred he

40

kept bottled up as best he could. "It's a proving place is what it is. That's what I was always told."

"Proving? For what?"

"A proving place for you and me. At least, for whomever arrives and for me, the one who always stays."

"You can't leave?"

Clevenger bowed his head at the truth. Pulling his broad Stetson down, it rested above his eyes, and all Holly could see was water. In his mind, he saw Clevenger on a three-masted ship. Saw the cresting waves and blustering gale. Heard the thunderous cannon. Clevenger stood at the rail with a musket and a sword. A British warship was close. Its men roared as smoke drifted across the battle scene—and across Holly's eyes—as he blinked and another vortex appeared. But he didn't run toward it this time. Could tell it is was just another disappointment. And sure enough, as the wind died down, the swirling mass sputtered out, spraying rock and debris along the gulley.

"I was on an American frigate, the USS *Chesapeake* out of Gosport, Virginia. Thirty-eight guns we had—or short cannon—the guns you just heard. We fought the British in 1813 in Boston. Ran up against the HMS *Shannon*, and let's just say, it didn't go so well. Shrapnel in the side sent me into the deep forever. I'd sailed before with Blackbeard, if you can believe it. Edward Teach, his Christian name, off the coast of Carolina, almost a century before. I was just as naive and dumb then. Manned the rail on the *Queen Anne's Revenge*. That had to be in 1718. Sailed for Godred the Black in the Hebrides in 1156. On the *Paralus*, during the Peloponnesian in 411. On the Hjortspring out of Denmark in 312 BC. Also, on the *Praise of the Two Lands* in Egypt. Before there were even years to name them. I'm sure there were other ships in-between, all lost to memory. I've drowned maybe 30 times. Over and over. I was always better with the blade than the musket. But of course, the muskets came long after my first dozen lives."

Holly's first glimpse of it all had his heart racing, when Clevenger in his youth was about to take the blast to end his life. Or one of his lives. But now, Holly's skin shivered to hear it all laid out over and over again. The drownings. The deaths. The bodies lost and returned. And he wondered if somewhere he'd drowned before, too? Was that his lot to suffer like Clevenger? Was that the big secret? We all got only one death to relive forever in different lives, in different times?

"No. I know what you're thinking. It's all different for everyone. That I'm sure is a rule. The dead die on their own, each their own. Some like me return over and over to get it right. Maybe I've just never gotten it right?"

"Gotten what right?"

"Why, dying, of course. It's just as important as living. No, sir, death isn't to be stumbled upon lightly, or overlooked. At least, not the right death. It's a process just like life. Maybe more so. Maybe more," and Clevenger stretched his hand out again. Turning it left and right, he marveled at the reaction of his shadow. The precise timing of it. The comfort. *Yes*, the comfort of it all. "To be comforted by a shadow?" he said. "Does that seem odd? Probably—considering you've had your shadow your whole life, and it was always there for you when you looked. At least, when it was bright out. So you've never lost it and can't know what it means."

"What could it possibly mean?"

"Comfort. Connection. It means there's a depth to my body again. To my time. One I haven't had for as long as I've been here. Now I don't feel so flat. Confined to this pattern. There is change and it is good and I've not seen that before here. Not with all the others who've stumbled through. And I just wonder if it's because of you? If that's something I should consider. Some proof to put on your side of the ledger."

Holly wondered at everything Clevenger said, as the strange man leaned forward and a single silvery tear escaped his eye. It rolled along his cheek, before arching into the air. Stretching out for moments and moments, they both watched as it fell to the gulley in a silent plop of liquid emotion. Flaring up with a sudden puff of black smoke, the dirt beneath it dissolved, and as Holly leaned in closer, beneath his feet, the smallest portal appeared like a window. And there—just below—was Nora! He could see her sitting on a rock by the river. There was a girl beside her, too, but he couldn't make out her face. The candle was lit, the one he'd left for her, and its light was as bright as the sun as he stared to see his love returned to him. To see her watching and waiting. The Shenandoah Staircase thundered its rushing current close by. Just north of where she sat. On the same rocks he'd careened through on his way to the confluence. Where the Potomac and Shenandoah met. Where he died.

11

THE CROWD STAYED ALL NIGHT AND WOKE when Nora woke. When the officer blasted his siren and came down from the road with two other officers, the panic ensued. Women grabbed blankets they'd sat on all night and the jugs of wine they'd brought, stuffing it in baskets and sacks. The three rowboats Nora had seen last night had really been a dozen (she couldn't tell how the crowd kept growing). Men and children stumbled on shore hurrying back to their wobbly boats, paddling with a passion she wouldn't have believed if she hadn't seen it. She could have cared less about the police. Had never known trouble herself, and didn't realize how one ticket could send each person into a downward spiral, furthering the poverty that kept them destitute to begin with. The candle was hope to them. A hope inscribed in their heart of hearts—each for them to know what they needed most—and the police didn't need anything. Just to harass. To scatter the hopeful. To lord over whatever kingdom they thought they'd carved out for themselves.

"Alright, now." The policeman from last night had made it to the clearing and grabbed the first person he saw. Fanning out, the two other officers charged through the brush with their batons. They swung at men and women as they fled in all directions. A few they struck in the legs fell where they ran, and as Nora watched it—dumbstruck by the suddenness of it—Juney grabbed her hand.

"They can't touch us, they can't," Nora insisted.

"Are you watching what I am?" and Juney shook Nora to her feet. The candle had stayed lit throughout the night. Not a drop of wax had fallen, and as some folks were still struggling to pull themselves from the trance it wove, Nora held it out and even the wind rising across the river couldn't waver its steady pulse. Folks had scattered, but still looked back to catch any last glimpse of the light they needed even as the police closed in. "I can't get caught," Juney added. "I can't."

"But we didn't do anything." Nora was certain they hadn't done anything wrong. They'd merely congregated on the banks and stayed close to the light. Some folks had stayed up not sleeping a wink, while Nora had fallen in and out of a slumber that was unlike any she'd ever had. And either by the warmth the rock had absorbed all day in the sun, or by some other force, she'd felt perfectly fine as the night frost came in and the wind whipped harder and folks shuddered beneath the coats and blankets they'd brought. She dreamed in the moments between waking, when she'd shift her legs and see another person shuffling closer to the candle. Like the solitary man who stood throughout it all, his hand on his heart, mumbling to some lost memory. When she did return to sleep, she saw an open plain. And wings. *Her* wings. They were stretched behind her, and the eyes of a million faces shined upon them. They were blue and iridescent and vermillion and mauve. Colors the likes of which she'd never known. All the sparkling eyes from all her many wings were focused on something that she couldn't see. Something she knew was there but still out of reach. And no matter how many steps she took or how hard she strained, she could never get any closer to it, whatever she needed to touch.

"My grandmother died two nights ago."

"I'm afraid I'd forgotten you'd told me."

"Meaning I don't know where they'll put me if they catch me," and with that, Juney had Nora moving. And talking. As the police lined up the ones they'd caught, Juney had Nora headed down along the Shenandoah. As Juney picked out the path, jumping from rock to rock, Nora would follow. When a voice called for them to halt, Juney knew it was the policeman from the night before, and turned Nora toward the woods. "I told you about the eyes the dead man gave her."

"*Yes*," and Nora's eyes sparkled with tears at mention of the dead man. Juney saw it and knew this was the key to keeping her moving.

"He was someone I'd never seen. Someone I found not far from here. I'd been to see Doc Fenzel about my grandma. There was nothing left to do but wait, but I thanked him anyway for his time. Then I felt it. Or rather—*saw* it. A strange wavering almost like a barely visible wing above the trees. I just knew I had to follow it. To see."

He was following them. Juney looked and the officer had left the other two to deal with the folks they'd caught. The two officers were kicking at pebbles now and then and writing down names, ages, and occupations (if there were any). The other officer was jogging along the rocks. He'd reached the point where Juney had turned Nora toward the woods, and then Juney couldn't see anything. They were under the branches, following a faint trace in the undergrowth. Juney had been down this far just the other day, when she'd followed that barely visible wing, teasing her on. That was when she'd met the dead man; he'd stood astonished and inert. Like he needed something to get him moving again. So she'd touched his cold, dripping hand.

"*What did you see?*" Nora had stopped as Juney pulled and tugged her hand, but couldn't get her to budge.

"Hush!" Juney crouched behind a thick fern and by either realizing they were being chased, or in following the humming instinct of her body, Nora knelt down, too. Juney heard the officer crunching atop pine needle and leaf, but he'd slowed from his earlier trot. It was all shadowy under the branches. Roots and rocks were scattered about, lumbering like the moss-covered limbs of some forgotten monster—but still the candle burned. "Jesus, it's gonna give us away." Juney nodded at the light, but Nora couldn't blow it out even if she wanted to (and her body certainly didn't want to). She couldn't release her hand from it either, though when the officer sounded not ten yards off, creaking in his leather boots, Juney had the idea to cup both hands around the light. "Oh," she said and closed her eyes. The warmth of it had burrowed into her body just like that, in being so much closer. She saw the dead man plain as day, when they'd stood on the riverbanks not thirty yards from here. His wide blue eyes returned to her. How they focused on the rapids and rocks, and she just knew they'd come out easy as pie, before leading the man home, to her blind grandmother, so she wouldn't be afraid anymore. So she could look at Death when it came. Stare it right down to its core.

"What do you see? What? You have to tell me." Nora needed anything the girl could give, any indication about Holly's eyes and what the girl's grandmother had seen through them.

"*Psst. Psst.*" A small hissing noise startled Juney from where she'd been in the light. Opening her eyes, she saw Rutherford B. Haze standing not ten feet from them, shaded by an oak. Juney knew his scuffed boots anywhere and touched Nora's cheek, so that she could see they weren't the only ones other than the officer underneath the brush.

12

HOLLY DUG WITH HIS FINGERS AND FEET. He scraped with a tree limb he found. Then he dug with the flat edge of a rock he'd uncovered, throwing all the dirt and debris back as quickly as he could pull it out. "*Nora!*" he screamed, and his voice echoed along the gulley before quieting into silence. There was only his breathing then. His breathing and the sounds of digging and Callous snorting to watch the maniacal rage in the man. He couldn't keep up this pace, but did. For an hour. For two. Digging almost six feet down, till the top of his head stood level with the rocky gulley.

"How?" Clevenger spoke and Holly didn't hear. Didn't want to hear. Didn't want to think about anything other than Nora's face. That shining instant. That glass portal. His world reduced to digging down for another glimpse. Of kneeling now when the rocks were tougher to dig through. Or using his chipped fingernails to edge around another buried stone. Another tree limb. *A cup?* He found a clay cup and stopped. Held it up so Clevenger could see. "Well, now. That *is* interesting."

Holly reached up to place the cup on the edge of the hole. It was a bit cooler where he stood, and he shivered when he jumped up to get both hands on the lip of the hole, before scrambling up like getting out of a swimming pool at the YMCA. Scraping the cup free of dirt and caked-on mud, he handed it to Clevenger who, unbeknownst to Holly, had a monocle underneath his shirt. A monocle he placed in his eye before raising the cup for inspection.

"I was going to ask you how it all happened," Clevenger said. "How one tear of mine brought out the portal like that. A looking glass of death into life. But now you've given me something else entirely to consider."

"Is it worth anything?" but then Holly remembered he was dead, and it wasn't like near the track. Where he'd pawn a watch during one of his losing streaks, and wouldn't tell Nora or explain how certain silver pieces from her family heirlooms might disappear for a whole week, only to be returned when he'd win at poker or on a longshot horse. Nora. He'd seen her. Clear and determined, sitting by the water. *The water right here!* and he looked at the gulley, at the inverse image of the world on the other side of the portal. It appeared so briefly, and he had it in his mind to grab Clevenger down from Callous and beat a few more tears out of him just to see if it would work. He was a short man—Clevenger. Holly had never seen him not on Callous, wrapped in a ruffled shirt and jacket. A pack with some indeterminate objects was slung across his shoulder. And why had he cried to begin with? *Ah, the shadow.* Holly looked as Clevenger inspected the cup, and the shadow of the man and mule stretched out beneath them in the dirt.

"It's Byzantine, I can tell you that. Probably from Constantinople. Not sure of the year. From the 1300s maybe," and with a swift dip of his torso, Clevenger swung the sack around and stuffed the cup inside. "Sometimes we'll find things. Trinkets. Objects we wouldn't expect to still be here. But digging down. Now that's an idea I hadn't considered. Through all the layers and centuries."

"We?" Holly looked up and had to shade his eyes, the light had grown more intense for an instant.

"The ones before you, of course."

"*Who* were the ones before me? And what did they find?"

"Well, there was Shama, a witch from Salem, drowned in 1692. Came straight away and found a wooden top that spun with a twist of her fingers. She was accused of killing a child. Not hers, mind you, but I always thought it interesting she found what she did. How it all syncs up. After you think it's nothing but waste. All the dirt and dust, the silence and emptiness. And that she found it so soon after arriving. Sometimes it takes decades. Though who could ever tell," and he shrugged at the sky. "I was in-between lives then. Have always been moving from life to death, to back here on Callous. Always on Callous here, while on water there," and he pointed at the hole, as if to intimate the worlds he'd crossed between. "Before that Gonreal, from Spain. Drowned in 1492. Thrown from the *Santa Maria* by Columbus himself. He'd stolen the captain's quadrant after a few days without any stars, and demanded another course plotted, a different way. He was charged with mutiny and thrown into the depths. A length of rope tied round his legs. The same rope he found after one of those whirling vortexes spun to a stop. Remarkable, really."

"You move back and forth?"

"I do," and Clevenger winked at Holly, before flashing the first grin Holly had seen from the man. "The right death still eludes me. And there was Polonius, of course, from Athens. Long ago, on a boat in the Mediterranean. He'd been afraid to board with the others. Had cowered instead, and even struck an officer determined to get him to fight. Well, the officer took an arrow for his efforts. But was able to pull Polonius down when he went over. So Polonius, of course, found an arrowhead in the dust. I still have it," and Clevenger patted the sides of his coat, before fumbling in a pocket to produce the glinting obsidian point. "Rasputin was here too, maybe only a dozen years ago. Though it's hard to tell years anymore, but he was an odd one. Had all sorts of bullet holes and knife wounds, and arrived without a boot. Just one. Told me the other was on the ice below a bridge in St. Petersburg. He always spoke in soliloquies about future events and was always wrong. Time meant nothing to him in life and meant nothing to him in death. I suppose that's why we found a pocket watch still ticking on a chain without any hands. A watch that never needed winding. If you listen, you still might hear it."

Clevenger turned enough so that Holly could see the sack on his back. Nothing else moved as Holly inched closer. Even Callous felt the need not to snort to hear the ticking presence. Which, sure enough, they heard—a tiny heartbeat pacing the world of this realm. Pacing death. Pacing the moments Holly felt coursing through him, as he saw again the cup, and the rowboat on the rapids. The whiskey bottle he'd taken with him fishing. The one shaken from his hand once the bow caught on a hidden ledge, when the boat tipped up. And to someone watching from shore, it would have looked as if Hollis Pride was walking for the longest moment atop the troubled waters. Then, of all things, a bluebird appeared beside him warbling on his shoulder, as if to apprise him of his circumstances, and it had so confused him, he'd almost forgotten he was about to drown. Which he did. *That damn bird,* he thought. Though he could still hear time in that world ticking away. Nora's time. Stepping back, he kicked a pebble to think of all the things he couldn't do for her, and at once a vortex spun up beside the hole.

"Watch it now! Stand back!" Clevenger screamed and Callous snorted, gnashing his teeth. Holly was close enough to feel the spinning heat of the thing, as bits of rock and dirt sprinkled his face.

"It's changing!" Holly said and stepped close enough that the swirling current scraped his nose. And either with this touch, or by some other organizing force, the vortex grew denser, as bits of rock began to fuse, and a patella emerged. Then two femurs. Then a pelvis and spine. Holly blinked and a half-formed skull appeared without a jaw. But then Callous charged into the gulley and Holly heard the air move and watched a silver blade come crashing through the skull. Crumbling to rubble, the vortex dispersed, and Clevenger leered down at Holly waving a broad sword at his side. Bits of bone crunched on the trail, as the light above them flickered once and then twice, before sputtering out. The shadows had dissolved. The skeleton was gone. The light was out.

13

THE CAVE WAS NARROW AND DAMP AND NORA followed Juney who followed the boy. They spoke not a word until he'd led them another hundred yards from the opening. Such a small cleft in the rockface and shrubs, you wouldn't have been able to see it unless you'd leaned against it with your whole body and watched your own hand disappear. Even then, you might not believe the magical illusion the opening presented. There were dozens of mine shafts in the mountain, the boy told them. With maybe a hundred smaller tributaries running in all directions, and which spilled into a few natural vents like this. Something to bring the air in. To take it out. To conceal black bear and fox and bat and whatever else decided it was as good a place as any to hide away in.

"Even the Virginia Cavalry during the Civil War," Rutherford B. Haze said, and his words echoed against the wet limestone walls. "Colonel John Mosby is what my daddy told me. A few miles north. I've been inside it; a man on horseback can just squeeze through. Then it widens into a space that could hold almost 120. Mosby hid his raiding troops there, whenever the Union chased him. Pretty swell, huh?"

"You came all the way down here from the ridge?" Juney and Nora had made it into a small clearing where Rutherford had stopped so they could gather their breath and listen. They'd heard some pattering noises behind them when they'd first entered, but weren't sure if it was an animal startled by their presence, or if it was that stumbling officer. Though Nora doubted the wide breadth of the man could make it into such a small opening to begin with.

"I almost never come down."

"Let me guess. You heard something? Or saw something?" Nora held the candle and Rutherford looked at it and then looked away as if it weren't anything to him. Just another candle. He held one, too; it'd burned almost all the way down. But he didn't need too much light to maneuver, being so used to it.

"No, my father talked with someone who heard there was some kind of to-do at the river. Near the confluence. I was just curious is all. To see if it was still happening."

"And this candle doesn't mean anything to you?" Nora held it closer to the boy, and he smiled at her like they might have been strolling through a park somewhere on a sunny day. There may have been church bells tolling and picnic tables covered with fresh-baked apple pies.

"Yes, it's a candle, mame. Is there something else you want me to see? If so, just point it out."

Nora stood still and watched the boy. He didn't need anything like all those others who'd gathered on the banks. The ones who stared at the candle like there was nothing else in the world that mattered. In fact, her body felt content standing beside him. It had no urge to rush off, now that he'd led them away from any trouble she could feel. Her body told her to rest. To ease into the presence of this boy who had something of Holly's lingering with him. She looked and his hand had a warmth to it that she hadn't noticed before. A darker shadow hovered on his fingers even when she brought the candle as close as she could, and the boy looked up at her with a quizzical tilt of his head.

"Just checking is all," she said. The shadow on his hand had a beautiful rich ruby tint. Something that reminded her of rose petals and sleep. With a rhythm that marked the pace of life, marking the pace of this day. It was a feeling that seemed to stand out more now after the excitement of the earlier raid on the river. Her heart wasn't thumping anymore, but beat steady. And the hand of the boy was steady as well, as he shook the hot wax from his candle and leaned back from how close Nora had come to him.

"Well, if you're just checking, you don't have to worry, I ain't the Gray Ghost. Just call me Ruddy if you want. That was Colonel John Mosby's nickname—the Gray Ghost. Though I don't think we can make it all the way up to that cave. That's another two mile. We'd have to walk along the river, too, and I've got to help my father, so if you don't mind—we'll just start out again toward home."

"Where's home?" Nora looked, and Juney was already tying her shoelaces a bit tighter; she seemed to know the effort ahead wasn't as ordinary as the one they'd just completed. The girl. *Juney.* Inside the tight, narrow cave it was the first peaceful moment Nora had experienced over the past day and a half to contemplate the sound of the girl's name, saying it again in her mind. How Juney just rolled off her tongue. How it seemed to go on and on and never end. It was a nice name. With a sing-song quality to it. Almost as good as any name for a girl starting with an E that she could think of. She wasn't a complainer neither. No, sir. After everything they'd been through, Juney had been the one bringing Nora away from the police. Juney had been the one who'd startled her from her ignorance on the river, when she'd thought they couldn't touch her, since they hadn't done anything wrong. They'd defied the police was what they'd done. They'd only dispersed for a moment, until the big officer left. Then they'd all come back, and Nora hadn't shook the light out or dissuaded them from being there, and figured she'd be the one questioned for the disobedience of the whole lot of them.

"Mame?" Rutherford had his shadowy hand on Nora's shoulder, and the warmth of it broke her contemplation. "It's a good spell up now, is what I just said. Are you okay with going up?"

"How's that?" The walls were wet, and Nora could see each creamy drop seeping through layers of soil. Rutherford looked at her again and was speaking, but she had to shake her head to hear him.

"I said, 'Are you okay with going up?'"

"Inside the mountain?"

"That's right, mame. It's the only way to go."

14

HOLLY KICKED AT THE BROKEN BONES LONG AFTER Callous and Clevenger retreated to the gulley ridge. Long after the grayness became the regular state of affairs again in the air around them. And long after he sat in his hole again and stared, wishing that portal would return. Wishing he could see her again. His wife. Though why he'd found a cup beneath six feet of dirt to begin with, he couldn't fathom? And why was the image of Nora already dissolving from him? Pressing closer to the bottom, he hoped there was still some lingering scent of her. If the living world could come back. If only she'd come back and know how close they'd been. Just on the other side. But she was gone. And instead, he thought how nice it was to be somewhere Clevenger couldn't see, where he'd regained a bit of privacy. There was nothing private in the gulley. He walked and saw whirlwinds and ran toward them only to watch them disappear, and that was it. Clevenger told him odd things and only spoke whenever Holly pressed him on certain issues. But there was never enough about what he had to do.

"There's only one thing to do," Clevenger spoke, and Holly looked up to see Callous sniffing at the rim. Clevenger leaned far over the mule and clung to Callous's ruddy mane. "We have to find the origin of that light now that it's gone. We have to bring it back."

"It was Nora's. It was the same candle that girl gave me after I'd given away my eyes."

"The same girl sitting beside her?"

"You saw her, too?"

Stepping back, Callous had swung around sideways, so that Holly could see the same profile of them that he always saw, walking in the gulley.

"The girl. She had such magnificent hair, don't you think?"

Holly couldn't breathe. He'd heard that exact phrase before. The girl's grandmother had said it when she could see again. After his eyes had been plopped into her head, Holly had stood there as the dying woman sat bolt upright and pressed her hands to her granddaughter's face. Holly remembered a twisting tangle in the shadowy room. *The girl's hair.* As thick as cords of rope. Nora had somehow found her, and he wondered if she'd come across any of the other people he'd given parts to? Misericordia? The boy in the mine shaft? Holly could still see his own beating heart in the boy's hand. And the boy's grateful smile before he pushed the heart into his father's cruel chest before giving him the metal clasp in return. "The parts," Holly said. "Maybe Nora is being drawn to all the people I gave my parts to?"

"And all their paths are converging?" Clevenger added.

"Maybe the light draws them out?" Holly paused as all the pieces seemed to fit.

"Just like you brought the light to us." Clevenger pointed at the grayness hovering around them, and the three of them sighed, not to see their arms reflect a corresponding shape beneath them. "And it brought out the cup."

"But the bird's nest and the metal clasp," Holly continued. "I haven't the faintest notion about them. I just dropped them at Nora's feet before I was pulled up through the window." Holly watched Clevenger peer up through the binoculars for as long as he could, before he felt again the holes in his face and where his eyes had been. "But maybe you could cry again, and we could see if it works?"

Curious at the idea, Clevenger leaned over and let the binoculars dangle from his neck. "What shall I think about?"

"About all your deaths. And why you keep returning here."

"I haven't died the right way. That's why they keep bringing me back."

"But what's the right way?"

Callous snorted and cantered away, and Holly lost sight of Clevenger. There was a shuffling of hooves; Holly heard Clevenger whispering a soothing incantation to the mule, before Callous cantered back.

"I can't tell you," Clevenger finally said. "He won't let me."

"Who won't let you? Callous? The mule?"

"He says it's against the rules. But I say it's perfectly well within the rules, considering you gave us the light, as far as I can see."

"That's right." Holly sensed some momentum here, an advantage he might use for the information Clevenger wanted to tell, but which the mule refused. He'd given Clevenger and this realm light a respite from the grayness that Clevenger and even Callous abhorred. At least, Nora had given it to them by being so close on the other river—the living one. Though of course, he'd given Nora the candle that the girl had given him for helping her grandmother. It was all a little confusing once you stretched it out like that, the cause and effect. But you could conclusively say after adding it all up and following it to the end that Holly had given something to Clevenger, and the rules clearly stated: *By giving something he had to get.* The words flashed like newspaper print in his mind, and he smiled seeing it all so properly typed and presented to him. "I gave you something, so I have to get something in return. The candle, the bird's nest, and the clasp were all that I got for giving away my parts."

"And your name. Don't forget about your name."

"That's right. Nora gave me my name back by saying it."

Callous turned to look at Holly and bared his cracked brown teeth. Hissing, he spat into the hole. Holly looked where some of it landed and almost expected to see that portal open up again. But there was nothing. Only Holly wiping his brow and Clevenger whispering as Callous turned and cantered out of sight.

"CLEVENGER?" HOLLY HADN'T HEARD ANYTHING from the gulley for moments and moments. It might have been days, for all he knew. He'd been thinking of the cup. And whiskey bottles. He saw the racetrack whenever he thought of Callous trotting back and forth. How he loved to stand at the rail and watch the really big ones run. The jaw-dropping speed of the animals. Flying right there as all four feet came up and propelled them through the air. On some days, with a few whiskeys in him, and maybe a few winnings in his pocket—he swore they flew. Swore on his soul that as the horses flew out beyond him, the jockeys were the luckiest fools in all the world to feel the heavy bonds of gravity melt from their bodies. The pull of Earth forgotten. Foregone by the speed and spirit of the horse. *The truth of it all.* It was as true as anything he'd ever known, when since dying he'd seen firsthand how the world's laws and truths seemed more like suggestions. Or forms to be reworked however you saw fit. To him, the speed of a horse could overcome gravity, so there was no telling what antiquated rules man could supersede with a concentrated effort. "Clevenger!"

Nothing. Another unending agonizing moment.

Wind sputtered above the hole. But still Holly didn't stand. Still Holly didn't want to leave the last place he'd seen Nora. "Callous! You know he's right. I gave you something and now I have to get! Clevenger! You even said it! That's why they keep returning you here. They keep bringing you back to do it right. So, let's figure it out. Let's figure out how you can die the right way."

"That's not the *only* thing I have to do right."

Holly heard Clevenger's voice. It was smaller, even colder. He might have been beside the rim all this time, waiting, deciding what to say. But Holly could feel his own body holding him down, holding him closer to the dirt. There was something beneath him his body wanted to be near, and uncrossing his legs, he eased himself down to lie on his back—and as he looked up—Clevenger leaned above the hole, turned a darkened silhouette, and pulled a broad meat cleaver from the sack on his back.

15

NORA HAD FALLEN BACK ONCE THE CLIMB rose steeper and the sweat started dripping from her nose. Juney was more adept at the rocky steps and muddy trail, at the tight cutbacks and blind passageways slick with limestone, so Nora followed the girl. The same girl who'd led her from the police. The same girl whose name she kept repeating in her mind as they went. The same girl she marveled at, watching her move up and up. She was indefatigable. Never seemed tired or huffed and puffed like Nora, since Rutherford never said how close they were to finishing. But cool airy currents rushed down to them now and then, and gave Nora some relief. Though it wasn't enough. She hadn't had as much as a sip of water all night, and now her throat was dry. It rasped louder as she coughed. Some whiff of coal fire or smoke had reached them, and as the air became hazy, she'd only watched Juney then, and the back of Juney's magnificent hair.

It was like a jumble of rope—cut from different shades of brown and red and gold. Somehow the different curls moved in rhythm to her churning limbs. As her shoulders went up, so did each riotous wave, but somehow it worked. Somehow it danced and swayed together, and she remembered the dream she'd had of her own daughter's hair, and what it'd be like. How they'd sit combing the auburn strands until everything was straight and sleekly tamed. Her daughter wore ribbons in her hair, in the short bangs she'd asked for. The girl picked the color depending on the dress she wore. Yellow was her favorite. Yellow and then blue. Always corresponding with her mood. A bright yellow. An adventurous blue. And only rarely a mopey, sleepy purple.

"Juney?" Nora spoke, and she wasn't sure if the girl heard. Rutherford was farther up, but they could see his faint light and followed it around another tight bend, ducking beneath boulders and overhanging tree roots. "Juney, would you tell me about his eyes. About what your grandmother saw. I have to know."

"Light." Juney didn't turn. Didn't even slow down. "And since they were dead man's eyes, I'm guessing the light was special. But I needed her to see the world to come. That's what I hoped and prayed for. She was so scared. And had been for weeks, after she took ill. When she stayed in bed and withered away from the strong woman she'd always been, raising me by herself, running a hen house for eggs, tending the garden, with the baking she did, the needlework and sewing. She was scared. And it was the first time I'd ever seen her like that."

Nora watched Juney's short, confident strides. Her overalls were scuffed at the bottom above her black and white saddle shoes. But Nora could see the overalls had been mended here and there; they'd been cared for. *Juney* had been cared for. Her shoes held a high polish, even though the events and lengths they'd traveled had dulled some of the shine from them. But the girl wore the practical love of her grandmother like a badge of honor, and to hear her tell how her grandmother had been scared—a woman who gave such love and confidence to the girl—shook Nora's rhythm. Pausing a moment, she rubbed her arms, shivering.

"She'd lost almost thirty pounds by the afternoon I saw the dead man, dripping and silent and stunned by it all. The police were laughing about something. I could hear them out on the rapids. But when they unstuck his foot from the rocks, from that other body of his, the one onshore could move again and followed me. I'd grabbed his hand as easy as anything. I wasn't afraid. Could tell it was where I needed to be. That he was the one to show her it wasn't scary at all. I also wanted her to see me once more, before she passed. She had cataracts for years. Glaucoma. They'd gotten so cloudy she could only see edges. Glimmers of light and color. She loved my hair and wanted to see it again and told me so. But she also wanted to see farther along the path she was headed. The one that took her not less than an hour after he left. I gave him that candle you carry so he could continue. I didn't know what he could see out of those empty sockets."

"Holly. His name is—*was*—Holly. My husband of eight years."

"Yes, mame. I kind of figured he was with how you are with that candle. I'm real sorry for your loss."

"And I'm sorry for yours," and Nora took a moment to compose herself, wiping the tears. "But it gives me comfort to know he came to you when you needed him most. And that he gave away his eyes. Without a word. Jesus, I didn't even know that could happen. That it was possible. That the dead could come back and do things like that."

"I just felt it was right as soon as I saw it. There was a wind rising above the woods. Something beckoned me. And when I saw him, a dead man standing right near where he'd just died and where his body was still not dry from the rapids pounding on him..." Juney hesitated, realizing she'd spoken a bit too closely to the wound in Nora's heart. Stopping, she turned to Nora in the close tunnel. The candle held between them flickered, as if to say: It's okay what you described. *It happened, didn't it? Keep going.* And as Nora smiled down at the girl, Juney turned and started again.

"I can't tell you what she did see. Just what she told me. Or rather, what she said. I sat beside her as she spoke in a stream of words. Sometimes she thrashed in her bed sheets. Sometimes she hummed and cried out. The doctor gave her medicine for the pain, but it wasn't enough. '*It's never enough,*' she said. 'To know the world is passing and to be upon it and to see it go and know you cannot change it. You cannot change what they've already set down in stone for you to live and see. But there are birds. There are birds and soft breezes in the trees. And a sudden scent of rose.' I was holding her hand, because I could sense it. My body felt it just as it feels the slick rock beneath us. She was going in. All the sudden she was quieter, hushed. *Reverent.* All the wind I'd heard moving the elm branches in the yard, brushing the shingles, scratching the house, had stopped. The railroad, the trains we always heard blasting through at night, at 3 am, at dawn, all ceased. 'Stillness,' she said. 'Stars. A red roan far off in a meadow of marigold and rue. Flowers, Juney . . . Oh, how I love them! And the light. Don't ever lose the light!'" Juney had stopped. Her words had captured Nora's thoughts and Nora hadn't realized she'd walked like that, listening as they climbed the last stretch. Ruddy stood at the top of the tunnel, a shovel in his hand. A cartful of lump coal stood glistening in the kerosene scent of a burning lantern. Voices were louder. Approaching. Nora looked at Juney.

"Was that it? Her last words. About light?"

"And birds. A bluebird, in particular. Singing."

Juney took Nora's hand, the hand that Nora held the metal clasp in. It settled in-between their palms. Juney didn't even bother asking what it was. Just held her. She hadn't told anyone what her grandmother had said in her last moments, and wouldn't ever again.

16

CLEVENGER LUNGED WITH THE CLEAVER ONCE, TWICE, swinging in the air. Then reaching down into the hole, he swung again so close, Holly heard its sharp edge slice an inch above his belly. Callous must have been down as flat as possible to let Clevenger lean over as far as he could without falling. Holly had not seen the man's eyes this close. But they were silvery. The green circles were edged with the slightest quivering line. They were small too, his irises, as if the grayness had diluted all the rage into the piercing green shade held at the center of him.

"You don't have to do this!" Holly cried.

"Oh, but I do. Callous told me. Callous knows everything. And he never forgets."

"Your mule?"

"Bigs sent you here because you gave away parts without knowing. You meddled in the order, and the order is all we have. It's what we follow."

"But I didn't know; I didn't hear the calling."

"Didn't hear the calling?" Clevenger leaned back as Callous snorted to hear Holly lament the calling voice or music he'd missed when he died. All he remembered was standing on the banks and the girl grabbing his hand. *The girl.*

"The calling tells you who you are. It lays forth your path—and your path alone. So, you see. You are out of order. You've meddled too much. That's why you're here. To set the order straight. I didn't mention it before, but most who come here . . . don't make it out."

"Most?"

"Well, really *everyone* who comes here ends up as..."

"Bones?" Holly remembered the skeleton resurrecting itself. Somehow by digging down and sending up debris, he must have gathered some scattered part and added it to the discarded bones and dust he'd trudged on with his soggy boots. The gulley, he now realized, wasn't made of dirt—but withered parts.

"Bones," Clevenger said and slumped down on the rim, resting the cleaver on his hip. He'd already dismounted Callous. *The mule.* Was the mule in charge here, Holly wondered. The mule didn't snarl or spit now, didn't bare his disgusting teeth. But just stretched up to his full height and stared down into the hole, staring into Holly, as if staring right through him into his cleft chest. Past the snapped ribs, the separated flesh and organs. Deep into the empty cavity that once held his heart. Holly could see the mule's nostrils flare, sniffing something nestled inside him. Sniffing the raw, meaty scent of all the parts still left to harvest. "All the bones are dust mostly. You've seen them. Seen the whirlwinds kick up." Clevenger leaned back on his knees and waved the cleaver as he spoke, gesturing along the gulley. "It's been like that since before I was assigned. Bones through and through. They come and are judged, are allowed to balance their deeds. But they never balance their deeds to the right. Even after giving some of their parts away before reaching here, they don't balance to the right ever. And then I harvest." Clevenger took his thumb and forefinger and pinched the cleaver's blade in a long, slow gesture. "I didn't mention before, but I was a cook on all those ships (when I wasn't being blown from the rail or dragged to the depths). I chopped the salted pork. Readied the chickens and lamb. I did all the butchering and was quite good at it. I suppose that was the one skill they sought in me and which kept me returning here to do my work."

Holly understood. Clevenger didn't have to say, didn't have to utter the cruel words. Holly felt along his own face. Felt his nose and ears and chin. His hair was close-cropped and blonde. His skull was normal-sized and didn't have anything wrong with it, as far as he knew. His legs and arms were intact. His hands, ankles, knees, and feet. All his organs were as clean and healthy as when he was a child. (Though his liver might have been the only thing distressed a bit, from the whiskey.) But his teeth. He moved his tongue along his teeth, the bottom and top set. He had such fine teeth, small and aligned, and he'd never once had a cavity or had one pulled or replaced, and he prided himself on that. It was something he liked to work into conversation now and then. His teeth. Would he even lose his teeth?

"Everything can be bartered for with Bigs. I give him what he needs, and he gives me another chance. Another life." Clevenger shook his head as if following Holly's thoughts, and then smiled, as his own pristine teeth somehow sparkled in the grayness. Of course! Holly had wondered what was off with the man after first seeing him. An inkling of it had kept his mind reworking his appearance in the back of his thinking. Like a constant unconscious calculation. His features—they were perfect! The man's nose was fine and sharp, his eyes were green, yes, but perfectly circular. His ears weren't too big. Didn't stick out too far. His chiseled chin had a cleft like a silent movie star. Even his neck wasn't dust-stained or wrinkled, but smooth and swanlike in its beauty. But the sum of those parts didn't make the man particularly attractive. It was actually more the opposite. He looked like a hodge-podge of rearranged parts. Something made of putty that a child would construct. He had the perfect pieces, but they were a quarter-inch too close in some aspects, or a quarter-inch too far offset in others.

"Of course," Holly understood. "So he keeps giving you another chance to drown."

"I suspect it's his idea of a joke."

"And, obviously, you take the prized parts for yourself?" Holly touched his nose, rubbed a dusty finger along his chin.

"Well, that's my answer to the joke. First dibs. Handsome, wouldn't you say?" and Clevenger turned a profile, took the Stetson from his head, and beamed. "I took this from a young Turk who came through not too long before you. Terrible man. Murderous. With pride and greed like nothing you could believe. But his nose! My God. Just look at it!" Clevenger leaned back to flaunt the shape of it, before facing Holly straight on. With his finger he touched the nose's fine bridge, and then flared the delicate nostrils. "Just tell me it isn't the most perfect nose you've ever seen." Popping the nose from his face, he held it in his hand with a satisfaction and smiled so Holly could see the nasal cavity and holes in his face, before tossing it down. "Careful now."

Holly had to sit up to catch the nose. But when he did, he inspected its angular precision and marveled at its loveliness. Holding it up beside his own, he imagined how he'd look with it, and quickly saw the improvement. The elegance would have served him well at the track. Might have stood him a bit more credit with the boys whenever he fell behind a few hands. Handsome fellows always got the benefit of the doubt. Were always patted on the back after losing and encouraged to try again. Even sometimes tossed a few easy hands, winning the meager ante to keep them happy. To stay just about even.

"It's perfect." Holly held the nose up, but Clevenger nodded sternly at him.

"Not like that. Don't throw it. I shouldn't have thrown it down to begin with."

Callous whinnied at Clevenger's words. And either with the knowledge that the mule was in charge here, or having finally discerned the inflection in the beast's noises, Holly swore he heard the mule laughing at Clevenger. Chiding him.

"I know; I know it was stupid. Don't you think I know that? I was just excited to show it off." As Clevenger argued with Callous, he set his cleaver down, before lying on the rim and leaning over as far as he could to grasp his most prized possession. In an instant, Holly saw the binoculars dangling from Clevenger's neck, and grabbed them. Screaming, Clevenger fell headfirst into the hole and reached desperately for his nose as Holly stepped up off the man's crumpled body into the gulley.

17

RUTHERFORD STOOD BESIDE HIS THREE SISTERS, April, May, and July. Beaming proudly, the boy looked more like a father to them than the man who lumbered out with his broken-toothed smile, his shoulders slumped, his gait wobbly, but determined. Nora saw the glimmering shadow on his shirt at once. The spot where his heart thumped steady and healthy and knew in her bones it was Holly's. That was why the dead husband who'd come back hadn't given her his heart. He hadn't been able to. Not with that gaping hole in him. *This man.* Looking at him, Nora had the urge to grab the shovel at Ruddy's feet and dig Holly's beating heart from the man's chest. Her hands ached to hold it. To feel the warmth and rhythm of her love beating right there for her. She would hurry with it then to Miss Misery. For surely, that woman would know how to preserve it, to keep it beating for as long as Nora needed to hear it, just to be near it.

"Mame?" Juney felt the gravity in Nora's limbs, saw how the candle had already inched closer to the man. Donald was how he introduced himself. Saying to them he'd heard there was some to-do about that candle, and tilted his head to look at it like how a dog tilts its head at an unseen sound. "Just looks like a candle to me," was all he could say. The need in him was already filled. The trance of the thing held nothing. So he rummaged then in the shed for a cup of coffee for Nora and a glass of cider for Juney. "You know he needed it, don't you?" Juney said, sipping the cider.

Nora looked into Juney's small eyes. Her lips sticky with cider. The girl knew so much. Knew everything Nora felt and thought. So why shouldn't she know about the heart, too.

"Look at Ruddy's face." Juney pointed to the boy lifting a bucket of coal, before tumbling the dusty clumps into a wheelbarrow. "You couldn't see it in the tunnel." The boy had a mottled bruise running along his left cheek in the shape of a fist. Donald's fist. "And the girls." Juney pointed and Nora's body flinched at the sight of them standing in line. All three the same size. All three dressed in frayed dungarees and denim shirts. Triplets. Their blonde hair as straight as could be and coal dusted. Something deep within them had been touched and stained by Donald. This had happened over the last five years of their lives like clockwork, she could tell.

"Until it stopped. Just recently," Nora understood.

"Do you see it, too?" Juney stepped closer to the girls and the three of them smiled their little faces up at her. There were warmer and safer shadows now lingering on their arms, their chests—over everything Juney could see. Nora saw it now and realized then that Juney still needed something, too. She'd known this in her body because the girl had been drawn to the candle, but it hadn't registered until that moment. Not until she saw the girl smile and tease the triplets as she asked them what their days were like. If they ever went out and played in the sun. If they had dolls and books and crayons to draw with. She hadn't seen them in school for many months now. And when she did, it was only for a day or two before they disappeared again. *What did Juney need?* Nora wondered, and sipped her coffee.

"I didn't mention it before, but Juney said something about it in the cave when you were wandering," Rutherford said, stepping closer to Nora.

"Wandering?"

"Yeah," and as Ruddy smiled, a kerosene smell wafted off him and Nora had to cover her nose before getting used to the dense, syrupy scent. "Wandering in your thoughts, I mean. I had to touch your arm to bring you back. But then she told me what it was that had you so concentrated. Because of the dead man. I saw him, too. He came here when I was loading the cart. When Mercy wouldn't move for the life of her. Almost as if she was waiting for him. Or smelled him. That she knew what we needed before I did."

"And who's Mercy?"

"Our mule."

Nora hadn't registered the animal. Shadows were drawn along the lengths of the mine shaft—but then closer to the shed where they lived—a wooden stock pen came into focus. An auburn tail swished back and forth like a metronome. Something that set the pace and rhythm of this place. The mule was quiet except for the swishing tail and Nora hoped to at least thank Mercy for her patience, waiting on Holly as she had.

"I didn't know it was your husband, mame. Honest." Ruddy bowed then, bending before her as if in benediction. "He's everything to us now. Everything."

The girls must have heard, because they ran up giggling and smiling at the slightest mention of the man they'd been too afraid to look at when he'd been there.

"Why did he stop here?"

"I'll tell you why." Donald stood at the entrance to the shed. He'd heard everything and moved toward the pen with Mercy and opened the gate. Clucking his tongue, Mercy cantered about, before Donald led her across by the lead rope. "It was me he gave it to."

Nora stared at his chest and had another notion to reach into it, but Juney stepped beside her and touched her arm steadying her.

"I haven't been well in some time. Not since their mother passed." Donald glanced at the girls, and it must have been a sign for them, because they ran off to the shed giggling and grabbed each other in some game that made Donald smile and shake his shoulders laughing. Even Mercy bared her clean small teeth. "Emmy took ill in her lungs and didn't last long. Told me to take care of them as best I could, but of course it was easier to drink and pretend I was doing what she wanted." He paused, touched Mercy's nose, rubbed his hand along the mule's soft side, before grabbing for something on his belt loop. Something that wasn't there—the metal clasp he'd given to the dead man. "You can live in this world and not remember it. That's how I was. I didn't feel the world anymore. Didn't have it in me to feel and didn't want to even if I could. Your dead man did it for me though. He knew without me or Ruddy even asking. A man without eyes, seeing it plain as day. Can you imagine?" He patted his chest and kept his hand there.

"He always did have a way." Nora smiled and leaned closer. "Do you mind?" She nodded at his chest and raised a hand. "I just want to feel it a moment. To hear."

"Of course," and Donald arched back before unbuttoning his shirt.

There was nothing else inside her then. Nora touched her ear to the man's chest, and the rhythm was Holly's rhythm, his easy sauntering stride. His quiet steady voice. His gentle familiar touch. Then all she could see was a long hallway. It was shadowed much like the mine shaft, before opening to a garden of rose and iris and daffodil. The colors exploded in her mind as she moved through each color and became that color as she moved. She was dancing, twirling her arms out in the steady rhythm, spinning now to be so close to her love. *To be inside her love. With him.* There was a galloping grace to it. Something was moving her closer, and as she adjusted her ear, pressing closer to the warm flesh, she could almost see it—the center of the man—the center of the heart. Holly's heart beckoned her on, pulled her closer to the sound where she knew there would be stillness after all the noise of living and learning and moving. Stillness complete and forever with Holly.

"*Nora!*" Juney was pulling her away. Mercy whinnied and Nora was confused and didn't want to rise up out of the rhythm, out of the heartbeat of love. But Ruddy and Donald were pushing them up on the mule's back and the mule was trotting down another tunnel as voices entered from the front. "The police! They're here! They just drove up asking for us."

18

CALLOUS WASN'T EXPECTING HOLLY TO CLIMB UP from the hole after watching Clevenger fall into it. But the mule just stomped his forelegs and stepped away from the sack that had fallen from Clevenger's back once Holly grabbed the cleaver. As Callous circled out wider in the gulley, Holly watched the mule and spun in time to the wide circuit the animal made, and a whirlwind sprouted up from beneath his boots. He'd kicked up some debris and half-expected to see another skeleton assemble into view. But as swiftly as it formed, the whirlwind settled into the gulley and Callous had loped back a full fifty yards from the hole. Then, turning with a grace Holly hadn't expected, the mule bared its cracked brown teeth and glared at him.

"You know I'm right," Holly said. "You know I brought light to this place for as long as it was here, and by rights, I must get something in return."

"Careful." Clevenger was on his feet, and Holly could hear his creaky voice rise from a foot below the rim. "He's not much of a negotiator."

The cleaver was much heavier than Holly expected. Its handle, a white ivory sheen, seemed made from polished bone. From part of a femur? he wondered. Or a jaw?

"Tell him I'm right."

"I already did."

Holly looked down and the top of Clevenger's head was sprinkled with dirt. A line of blood trickled from his forehead to his eye.

"I was going to be sent back right after," Clevenger said, and he made a chopping motion with his hand, and Holly knew what he meant.

"But I thought I had to be judged?" Holly said. "That my deeds had to be balanced to the right? Have I been judged then?"

"It might not mean what you think," Clevenger added. "Balance," and Clevenger pointed to Callous.

"No." Holly stepped back until his boots were at the rim's edge, now that he understood.

"Yes. Callous is the judge here. All who are sent must balance atop Callous if they are to be deemed acceptable. Then I can help."

Callous had heard it all and apparently didn't like it, now that Holly knew what was required of him. As if responding to a pistol, Callous charged as fast as any blue roan Holly had ever ridden or seen. All four of the mule's hooves came off the dirt and floated beneath him as his body rose and fell in a rhythm that held Holly enchanted. The air seemed hushed in this moment of grandeur, of stillness and speed. That was until Holly saw the distended shapes in the mule's left side bouncing and quivering as he raced toward Holly. There was only a moment for him to move, to jump up as if pulled by strings, the cleaver still clenched in his hand. Callous had leapt and—in time to the mule—Holly jumped and landed on the mule's back as Callous cleared the hole and galloped off, screaming and frothing at the mouth. Barreling down the gulley, the mule felt the dead man upon his back, sitting backward as dust and rocks spit out from the mule's furious hooves.

"Balance to the right!" Clevenger screamed and Holly understood at once. The mule's distended body pulled his center of gravity to the left, and so Holly—still seated backward, his boot heels digging into the mule's sides—leaned as far as he could in the opposite direction, even as Callous jumped up in a huff. Or turned in sharp wild angles, rearing up on his hind legs to try and throw the man to the dirt.

It was just like at the track. Holly had never ridden backward, of course, but he was able to find his stomach again. He felt the muscles in his torso and thighs clamping down. Flattening himself and leaning as far as he could, Callous grew tired from the effort, or was just teasing Holly into loosening his grip—but for some reason—Holly's voice had started counting. He called out the seconds he'd ridden balanced on the beast, and with each new second, the mule seemed to lose that much more of his strength. Having made one last turn, Holly sat upright, crossed his right leg over the mule's rump, and spun his body to face forward, where he could see the hole approaching. Fearing still the animal's anger, Holly placed his left hand on the beast's warm neck and rubbed down with his hand, patting the animal—his judge—until Callous stopped beside the hole and snorted.

"*Unbelievable*," Clevenger had jumped up and clung to the rim watching. "I've never seen light here before, and I've never seen anyone balance on his back. Not even for two seconds."

"May I dismount?"

"You tell me? Maybe you're my replacement?" Clevenger smiled as Holly sat on Callous, the cleaver still in his hand, the sack from Clevenger's back rumpled and dusted in the dirt.

Callous shook his head, twitched his ears, and let out the longest screeching whinny Holly had ever heard. It was all Clevenger needed to know.

"Astonishing."

"What?" Holly had slipped from the mule's back and—with an eye on the beast's hind legs—stepped around so he could see Clevenger more clearly. Holly had also grabbed the sack and had an idea about what he'd hoped to gain for bringing the light here. There was something he wanted to try.

"I didn't think it would be as easy as that. Trading places with you. Callous seems to like you."

"Like me?"

"It just took that balancing trick is all. And riding backwards, no less. Good show, man! Callous said you really know how to ride. *As if I don't?*" and Clevenger frowned at the mule for the insinuation.

"It felt so familiar," Holly said. "Like being home. But I don't want to replace you. Not in the least."

Clevenger didn't have anything to say to that, but watched with an air of interest as even Callous turned to inspect the swift movement Holly made in holding up the crumpled sack.

"But I would like the cup I found."

19

NORA COULDN'T HOLD ONTO MERCY'S REINS and the candle, so instead, Juney held the reins and sat in front. The child was warm nestled against Nora's chest, and as she settled in, a momentary feeling of comfort washed over her. In the almost complete blackness of the tunnel, Nora, for a moment, felt like she was riding home. That this was the way forward, and Holly was waiting for her on the other end. That Miss Misery would have tea and maybe some more of the bird's nest soup waiting as well. A blanket at the ready. Some toast with strawberry jam. That Juney would stay with them, and Nora wouldn't ever have to dream or wonder about what it would be like to have a child, to miss a life of fullness. She looked and the candle burned soft and steady, and Mercy seemed to know the way, turning around the tightest corners, cantering from side to side when vague boulders and old timbers reared up in the way. The woman and child moved in rhythm to the mule and felt safe to let the quiet of the deep stone and clattering hooves carry them on.

"My grandmother was all I had," Juney spoke and Nora let her. Didn't need to interrupt. "My parents were gone long before I could remember, right after I was born. I don't think my father had any brothers or sisters. There aren't any aunts or cousins to speak of. At least not in the vicinity. At least, not which Grandma ever mentioned. That's why I'm worried about the police catching me. About what they can do."

"They can't do anything. I won't let them."

Juney didn't turn or twist a muscle. Didn't want to remind Nora how she'd said the same thing along the river, and that she'd been wrong then, too. The police had just plowed through all those scared people; it'd been like nothing to them. Just like now. It was all wrong, and Juney wondered what it would be like if all these folks ever listened to her for once. Then she wouldn't have to explain to this woman that the police wanted to put her in a home. Probably state-run. An orphanage. *She was an orphan now.* They'd also probably want to take her away from where she'd grown up and lived and been happy. If they'd only listen, she wouldn't have to lead this woman on through God-knows-what cave to get to wherever they thought they were going. They'd have already left for some other life in some other town. A woman without a husband, and a girl without any parents. It was perfect. But Juney knew she still had a task to keep her here. Until it was done. "I still have to bury her," she said, as casual as if she were listing off groceries.

"Is she still in bed?"

"Yes, mame. The coffin's been bought. So's the headstone. I just have to transport her to the cemetery above Harpers Ferry. I'd like to put her in her favorite dress, too."

Nora flinched at the realization—this girl was more of an adult than most folks she knew. She already had responsibilities of the dead weighing upon her, and now with whatever power the candle held, the police were after her, too. Nora had done all this, had brought this upon Juney's little worried head and tangled hair, and suddenly wanted to touch it. To touch the girl. To comfort her in some way. So, putting the metal clasp she'd held till then in her apron, she reached up and placed her hand on the girl's shoulder. Juney's magnificent hair were jostled a bit by the mule, and the strands that fell upon Nora's hand were as soft and lovely as gossamer, and it was all she needed to steady herself. "I can help you bury her. I'll help you change her, too."

"You don't have a car, do you?"

Nora didn't say anything. She was thinking about how they could possibly bring the girl's grandmother across the river and up the steep ridge Harpers Ferry was nestled into. She had Mercy though now, didn't she? Donald and Rutherford hadn't said it, but once they were on Mercy, Donald had touched his chest, and Nora could tell this was what he had to give for the second life Holly had given him. A trade. And maybe with Mercy, she could find a carriage. They could take the roadway, and then wind through the cobbled streets, up through Harpers Ferry, with someone waving the cars by in their procession. She could see it all in the sparse light in front of them. The scene and stately honor of bringing the girl's grandmother to her final resting place. She would be helping the girl in some tangible way after all the trouble she'd brought her. She had a mind to turn the girl around right then and tell her, when a strong windy gust blustered through the narrow cave and the candleflame—the one that had been so steady for so long, and which she'd never had a second thought about—flickered in front of them, wavering back and forth, before sputtering out.

"Well, that's no good," Juney uttered in the sudden darkness.

Mercy stopped as soon as the blackness became absolute. Above them, the last glints of light rose against the walls, and in that last moment, Nora had seen the water-stained rocks shine like glass. She thought she'd seen her face reflected in them, and then all she could see was nothing. She held the candle closer and couldn't even see it, an inch from her face.

"What does that mean?" Juney had turned enough so that Nora could feel the warmth of her face close to hers.

"I didn't think that could happen. I wonder if it means something about Holly?"

"Or us?"

Nora was certain it meant a change had come somewhere, in some world— either the one she and Juney and Mercy existed in, or the one that held Holly. Clucking her tongue, they could hear Mercy nod her head as if in agreement, sniffing the motionless air, before starting off again, but slower. The mule knew the way even without seeing. Ruddy must have run her through this cave any number of times as he retraced the trail that Colonel John Mosby (the Gray Ghost) had taken in leading his men beneath the mountain. Because Nora knew they had to be like ghosts now, too, if they were to escape the police, to bury Juney's grandmother. To do whatever else her body compelled her to do, to make things right for this girl. Because her body was compelling her to stop now. To take the reins and pull Mercy up and maybe turn around right here in the tight cave. Her body wanted to head back to the river where she knew the candle would burn again. Where it had burned all night without hesitation, without even once flickering off like this. *Jesus, why had it flickered off?*

"It's okay," Juney spoke, and Nora's body unclenched from the tension that coiled through her. Juney had felt it, and was the adult again, easing the situation out. Making it right. "Just promise me, you'll bury her."

"Juney, I'm right here. We'll bury her together."

"You didn't promise me yet."

Nora saw the outline of the girl's magnificent hair. A tangle of shapes had come into focus. The girl was leaning over the mule and whispering into Mercy's ear. Nora could hear her faint fading voice. There hadn't been any sound for what seemed like ages, and now Nora breathed easier to see that something had brightened around them. She heard someone else breathing, too. It was the girl. She'd turned in the brightening air, and Nora could see gleaming lines down her face. She was crying.

"Juney? What's wrong? What is it?"

"It's a brown full-length dress with cream piping on the sleeves. And the hat, the fascinator, the one she never wore but always wanted to. With a feather mesh and a stuffed cardinal on top."

"For your grandmother?"

"She wanted to wear it to the track but never had the courage. To see the horses. To *promenade*, as she called it. She was always so shy."

A bend appeared before them, and after Mercy went around, there was more light. Nora squinted to see the bright pulse of it take up all she could see; she hadn't realized how dark it'd been, especially if such a small opening in the cave could do that, bringing in the faint afternoon, blinding her like this.

"Alright, mame. That's enough."

There was a hand on Nora. A man was pulling her off Mercy, and the light was a flashlight he shined in her eyes. Juney had already been pulled off and was being marched in front.

"*Juney!*" Nora screamed, but the officer didn't stop, and Mercy hissed and snorted, and a third officer grabbed the reins and pulled the mule back so that Nora could hear Mercy's hooves stomping in place like almost treading water, not able to move forward or back. She felt like she wasn't moving forward or back either. But she could still see one last glimpse of the girl. The tears on Juney's cheeks. Her hair alive and flared out like the candleflame Nora had watched for so long. The amber, gold, and red strands of it a living, thrashing animal in its own right. A bright bonfire to follow, to find always and forever as the officer led her out. "*Juney!*" Nora screamed again.

"Promise me!" Juney yelled back. "You still haven't promised me!"

20

HOLLY HELPED CLEVENGER UP FROM THE HOLE and was about to climb down with the sack, when Clevenger touched his shoulder. "Wait," he said. As he spoke, Callous nudged him with his nose, pushing Clevenger closer. The mule seemed directing some ritual here, something Holly hadn't expected. "In honor of balancing upon Callous, the Fifth Judge of the More-Troubled Drowned Dead (I know, it doesn't quite roll off the tongue), Callous has decreed you're permitted certain parts for your collection."

"My collection?"

"The collection of parts you need to continue. To ascend to the next level?" Clevenger raised an eyebrow, as if Holly should understand all this, before declaring a thunderous proclamation. "Eyes!" Pausing, Clevenger let the word sink in. Then with a subtle glance, Callous turned his broad, distended side, and Clevenger reached into the mule's belly. There wasn't any blood. Nothing spilled to the gulley, and Holly hadn't seen any opening in the mule to allow for Clevenger's arm, but there it was—the man in up to his shoulder. After rummaging about for longer than Holly had hoped, Clevenger pulled out two of the brightest blue eyes Holly had ever seen. "For bringing light to the realm, here are the eyes with which to see it."

As soon as Holly held the eyes, he felt the person they belonged to. Memory clung to each part. The man had been one of the nameless many who'd been placed here after his more-troubled drowning. The ones with an aggregate of sins piled against their good deeds. Unable to balance to the right to save themselves from falling lower. Falling to what—Holly couldn't even consider—but there was lightness in his eyes. An anticipation came over him. He'd place them within his head and see this realm for what it was, not for the shadowy edges and inverse shapes he'd grown accustomed to. And the man who still remembered these eyes might see it, wherever he was.

"Well?" Clevenger nudged Holly, who slid them into the sockets and staggered as he did, blinking. Even the dull grayness was blinding. The color had not been color before, but more a feeling, a drab shadowy contrast. Now he saw *grayness*—and loved it! Raising his hands, he felt the shade pervade his mind. It had a nuance he hadn't realized. Black and white mixed in different intensities down to the tiniest particle. The complexity was stunning, and if it wasn't for Clevenger clearing his throat to continue, Holly might have stood there for days reveling in the beauty. "For giving me feeling, for allowing me to see light and for realizing the rules were correct, and that I—that we—were wrong." Clevenger looked at Callous with a sideways glance, and Holly realized they must have argued about giving him something monumental for reminding them of abiding by the rules. "A heart!"

Clevenger reached again into Callous, and the mule shifted this time so that Clevenger could reach into the middle of the mule's chest. There came a sound then of a thunderous rhythm. The noise grew louder the closer Clevenger's hand came to all the beating hearts they'd harvested. "Not all are worthy, obviously," Clevenger said, as if answering Holly's thoughts. "Some pass through and their eyes are just wonderful, but everything else rotten. And some, well, some have hearts as pure as snow, and morals as warped as melted glass. But I believe this one will serve you well."

The beating heart was wondrous to see. Holly remembered his own and the bright pulse of it, before giving it to the boy. But his eyes had already been taken from him by then—so the heart didn't have anything like the red vibrancy held before him. It beat its steady pulse, and as Holly touched the dense muscle, the memory of running came to him. Feet ran leaping into air. Wind pushed past his face, his hair, his skin. He saw moonlight and dancing. There was movement and emotion, and as he placed it slurping into his chest, his ribcage grew over it. Then as his flesh resewed itself, he felt his body jolt in time to this new rhythm.

Placing his head on Holly's chest, Clevenger heard the resounding pulse and patted Holly's arm, before looking back at Callous. The mule was satisfied. Stamping his hooves, the ensuing dust cloud had Holly waving the debris from his eyes. *His eyes!* He'd already forgotten he had them and blinked until a few tears lined his cheeks. The tears reminded him of what he still hoped to do. Reaching into Clevenger's sack, Holly's hand passed across a host of shapes he didn't understand until at last, he pulled out the clay cup.

"I got to thinking," he said, "about all the other objects you mentioned, and that are probably still in there." Slumping the sack at Clevenger's feet, Holly knelt slowly, set the cup on the ground, before climbing into the hole. "Do you mind?"

Clevenger saw what he meant and handed down the cup.

"You said that each one who comes here finds something. How it all syncs up, when you think it's nothing but waste."

"Of course, the ones here find their special something, but usually they've given up by then. Still, I wait for them to find it, considering it reminds them of what they've lost. It's cruel, I know, but it usually does the trick."

"What trick?"

"Breaks them down, so when I raise the cleaver, they don't even care. They can barely stand on their feet by then, so to balance onto Callous would be impossible. It's like a waiver of rights, if you want to think of it that way. I ask them and they couldn't care less; they just want it to end."

"Well, I *don't* want it to end. I don't even want to think about it anymore. I just want to try something." Turning, Holly took off his jacket. The remarkable water he'd drowned in, from the Shenandoah, still seeped in his clothes and boots, even in his ears whenever he shook his head. Sometimes it came bubbling up out of his throat when he was about to speak. The portal had been opened by Clevenger's tears—by water. So, wringing his coat above the hole, he hoped it might open the portal, too, but was skeptical. He'd trudged up and down the gulley, and during all the steps he'd taken, a fine mist had sprinkled out from him, but no portal or glassy viewpoint appeared. And sure enough, after wringing out his jacket, the hole only became a muddy mess. Kneeling, he scraped with his flat rock and tree limb, and even with his own cracked fingernails. But after pushing up heaps of mud, the bottom still showed as dirty and rocky as before.

"My tears did it," Clevenger said. "Why doesn't your water work?"

"We're different, you and I. When you cried, you'd already bartered for another life, with Bigs and the boys. You were going back after you cut me up for parts."

"That's true." As Clevenger spoke, something was happening in Holly's heart. Blood was pulsing again through his flesh. The rhythm resounded in his ears—before rising higher—pulsing into a bright crescendo around them.

"I'm guessing your true tears about seeing the light, about the shadows it brought, had the effect we saw. It opened the portal to the true patience of my wife—Nora waiting by the river. The *other* river," and Holly pointed to the bottom. "But the cup changes things. The cup is something I found in this realm. It's a marker, a reminder of what I did wrong with my life. And if this is the inverse of that other world, with the river flowing below us, then the inverse of what I did wrong in that life would be right in this life, in death. It would be the correction."

Clevenger blinked at the possibility and looked at the cup, before climbing down beside him. "Jesus, how long were you down here thinking?"

"There's only one way to find out," and taking off his boots, Holly wriggled from his pants. "In life, I poured whiskey and water *into* myself; now, I need to pour it out."

"So you think the cup is your key, so to speak?" Neighing at Clevenger's words, Callous leaned above them, and Holly felt the mule's warm breath on his neck.

"Why else would I find it?" Holly looked back to realize Callous's calm, steady voice had echoed in his mind.

"I told you it just takes a little time to understand him, to hear." Holding the cup now, Clevenger poured the contents of one of Holly's boots into it.

"The other." Holly nodded as Clevenger poured out the second boot. "Now the pants."

"Really?" Clevenger held the damp, muddy pants as Callous whinnied to see the disgust on his friend's face. "Yeah, well you can do his underwear."

Holly shivered in his boxer shorts. His undershirt bulged above his chest—which beat louder as the cup filled—halfway now. His new heart was slightly larger than the old one. But he could feel the lightness of it rising, the buoyancy in his body as a floating sensation filled him. "Now the shirt." Clevenger wrung out the sleeves, the seams, the collar, until the cup was full. And by being full, curiously, the cup changed. The clay sides glistened like stained glass. Colors swirled in the depths of the design. Clevenger and Callous leaned closer to see blue obsidian lines, silver waving circles, and an umber outline of trees.

Holly's heart pounded as water gurgled from his mouth. His hair was slick against his skull, and snaking lines of water trickled down his chest, before spreading in a black puddle beneath him—a puddle he added to as he poured out the cup.

Colors were the first thing they saw. As an inch of water sloshed beneath them, the colors grew upon the surface. At first, they aligned themselves like circular bands. But as Holly stirred the edge, the colors swirled into a whirlpool, and Holly could feel himself teetering to fall in. In another moment, the colors merged, and a glassy portal appeared in the center. He could see the Blue Ridge right below him, and dipped his toe through the bottom. The river rushed close beneath.

"Holly?" Clevenger held onto his arm. But as Holly's foot went in, he couldn't hear anything in the dead world anymore. *There were birds!* They drifted close by and flapped their wings with an airy assurance. Then his other foot was in, and his waist, as the wind of that other world brushed his skin.

Screeching, Callous hissed at them to stop, but only Clevenger heard. He couldn't let go, even as his hands slid from Holly's arm. It was like Holly was dissolving piece by piece into a swimming pool. As Clevenger placed his hands on Holly's back, Holly laughed once before ducking his head under. Then all Holly could feel was resistance. The Shenandoah gurgled and popped in the valley, and his limbs all dangled in the air as if emerging from the bottom of a cloud. Far below, he felt a force pushing him up. Something was forcing him back into the same portal the dripping water was pulling him through. The water of the dead and the air of the living had met with such force, Holly was suspended. "Clevenger! Callous!" he screamed, but the man and mule only heard the portal gurgling as it tried to close, as all the water drained into the living world.

"He's stuck!" Clevenger cried, and pushed as hard as he could, but nothing. Only Holly's back seemed to keep the portal open. "Callous! Do something!"

Clevenger was stuck now, too, his hands sliding into the depths. The mule could see it all and understood another egregious undoing of the order was happening right before him. All on his watch. And without a final snort or warning, Callous stood from the hole, ran to the higher rim, turned with one last look at the dusty, dirty realm he'd governed for longer than he could count, before charging toward his friend. Leaping onto Clevenger's back, he let out one last defiant hiss, before all three—the mule, the butcher, and the dead man—slurped, dripping through into the living world.

PART III:
ABOVE THE CONFLUENCE

21

NORA FELT THE METAL CLASP INSIDE HER APRON click open from its closed position. It was loud and odd and as she reached for the clasp, Mercy paused beneath her. They were on the highway. They'd taken it down from Bolivar, the small town nestled above Harpers Ferry. She'd already made her statement about Juney at the police station, talking about the candle and the gathering along the riverbanks. Stating she hadn't done anything wrong, and Juney should be with her. None of it mattered. As they wrote her ticket and shooed her away, she hadn't remembered the clasp to begin with. She'd only rode Mercy. Had hugged the mule as they went, and followed the curving ridge until she spotted the dirt path that would take her to Juney's farmhouse. And now, as they made their way up, she couldn't stop thinking about the man. The one before Holly. The one Holly didn't know about.

It was someone she'd met when she was sixteen, just a girl working weekends at the soda fountain in Charles Town. A businessman visited once a month on his sales rounds. His territory covered the eastern panhandle of West Virginia, and down into Virginia and Maryland, along the Potomac. Selling girdles and bras and women's undergarments, if you can believe it, and Nora snorted to think of it, riding Mercy up through the trees. *Why now? Why did she see his face?* His mustache had tickled her neck whenever he bent close enough, ordering his root beer floats those Saturday nights. The track wasn't far off, and when she wiped the tables on the front sidewalk, she could hear the bell clang and the crowd roar for the big race. Moths fluttering in a swarming mass at the streetlamp. Those musty, humid August nights. She would only find out later that Holly was at the track, working the shed row. A stable boy, shoveling shit. Pitchforking hay. Doing all the upkeep and rotten jobs for a dollar a day. There was a motel the man stayed in. She could still feel the crisp bed sheets. Ironed and white. She didn't know why she'd done it with him, but it'd been her first time and felt like something from one of the radio operas her mother listened to, with all the drama of it and a motel room. That was why when Mercy finally made it up the hill, and Nora gazed upon the farmhouse with the dead woman in it, she knew it had been Holly's problem they couldn't have a child. She remembered the one she'd lost. On purpose. And rubbed her belly. The man spent good money on the herbs the woman concocted. Tansy, safflower, and wild celery all mixed with bitter water. *Terrible.* The month she spent between bed and walking past the garden to throw up so her mother wouldn't know. Holly never knew. She'd never told him. She'd never been able to. And sliding down from Mercy, she wiped a tear and spoke to the mule just so she could hear her own voice about it.

"We tried and tried, but still Holly never once wanted to ask a doctor. Said that was too much money to find out something we already knew. And that was when his drinking really picked up."

Mercy leaned closer and held her long head to Nora's side.

"I know," Nora muttered, as if listening to the animal's consoling voice. "It's just life. And I guess death now, too." Looking at the house, the screen door swung open in a sudden breeze, and then slammed shut as a few leaves scattered on the stone walkway. "But now Miss Misery says he had it in him, says I was wrong all this time. She says a lot of things, doesn't she?"

Mercy snorted and Nora laughed to hear the mule express the same feelings she had about that mysterious woman.

"She is an odd one, I guarantee. Still," she said and rubbed her belly. "The bird's nest soup? I wonder if it made me see things that were always there? If it let me feel things, too. Things she knew I needed to feel."

INSIDE THE DEAD WOMAN'S ROOM, Nora found the dress and hat laid out on a chair. The same ones Juney had described. "*Juney.*" Nora said the name and turned back the covers and held the scissors she'd already found in the den. This was not something she knew she would do, but her body had demanded it. Had found the scissors beneath a pile of envelopes on a desk. The scissors were heavy, and cutting the nightgown was easy. The cotton thread was so brittle it slid right off, and Nora swore it would have drifted into vapors if another breeze had passed through the room. But she was able to slide it off and place it on the chair. "For Juney," she said. "She'll want that, I'm sure. She'll want to know about everything," and she looked at the woman, at her eyes. *Holly's eyes.* The blue wasn't yet faded like she supposed it might. She'd thought the body would have been puffed up, too, from all the gases, but enough time had passed she guessed to un-leaven the body. Or maybe it was unnatural all the way around—and none of it was going as the natural order demanded? "I mean, Christ, she's got my dead husband's eyes in her head. Where the hell did her eyes go?"

Slipping the other dress on took some doing. She had to turn the body on its side and then pull the arms up before easing the dress down, straddling the dead woman as she did it, to gain some sort of purchase over the situation. All the while she didn't want to look into Holly's eyes as she did it. She didn't want to see him watching her from his world. Wherever that was. *Those eyes.*

"Jesus," she said and wiped her brow when it was done and the afternoon light had drifted down. The shadows racing away. It had taken her some time to wrestle the woman into the dress Juney said she'd been too shy to wear, but it did suit her for where she was headed. The coffin was in the living room, and Nora had dragged it along the floor beside the bed. Pulling the woman's legs down, she had to get behind her on the bed, using gravity in the process. Another round of tugging and teasing took a half hour before the dress looked as pretty as it had when she was on the bed. The hat was easy and fit with a few bobby pins after Nora brushed out her hair. "Her hair," and she recalled Juney's magnificent hair. The same hair Juney's grandmother had looked upon with Holly's eyes, and a tear escaped again landing on the woman's cheek. It smeared the makeup Nora had applied *liberally*—which the old woman probably wouldn't have liked—but in her condition, couldn't complain about. "There," Nora said and had to reapply some rouge and touch up the lipstick, but she'd done it. "For Juney."

"Well, I believe the makeup was largely for you."

The voice startled Nora—and when she turned—Miss Misery stood in the doorway, sweat lining her brow.

"You?"

"I had a feeling you'd be here. Saw it all depicted on your kitchen wall. I never do know where the visions will appear. You'd think after all these years I'd have a better handle on where and when to look. *Life.* It is a mystery; I swear. But I brought you something." Miss Misery took ahold of Nora's quivering hand—because she was either scared from the woman's sudden appearance, or exhausted from all the effort—but Miss Misery had to direct her to the living room window to see.

"How'd you know?" An old wooden cart with steel hoop wheels and wooden slat sides sat already hitched to the mule. The coffin would just fit.

"I was out in your back yard beneath the oak tree when a smell caught my attention. It had me walking all the way to the riverbanks where I suppose you'd sat all night. *Odd.* It was something I hadn't smelled in a few days and which I hadn't expected to ever smell again, at least not in this world. But there it was," and Miss Misery searched Nora's eyes a moment. Clenched her hand tighter. They'd been holding hands ever since Miss Misery arrived.

"The river?" Nora closed her eyes and could see it—at the confluence—where the Shenandoah was gobbled up by the Potomac. Just like how Holly had been gobbled up too, and she shivered to hear the rapids and feel the misty spray even as she swayed a mile and a half above it.

"All I'm saying is don't go down there anymore. There's no telling what you'll find."

22

HOLLY PLUNGED HEADFIRST INTO THE WATER. Bobbing up in his boxer shorts and undershirt, he watched as Clevenger fell through followed by Callous into the rapids beside him. Clevenger cried out once with a strange smile, before being pulled under, and Holly remembered the man couldn't swim. Even after all those lifetimes of drowning, the man had never bothered to learn, and he chuckled as Callous coughed out a snout full of water and came up beneath him somehow. So that as Callous stood, Holly sat upright on his back.

Above them, Holly watched the portal dissolve and a misty cloud appear where he thought they'd come from, but then Callous had risen with a nervous whinny, and Holly could only concentrate on his legs. They dangled and dripped water into the breeze as they rose into the air. *They were rising!* While on the banks, far below, he saw a woman whispering on her knees. She sniffed the air once and then twice, before her eyes rolled up into her head, and if she hadn't been kneeling like she was and her hair brushed back, he'd have guessed it was Misericordia, the woman from the woods, the one who'd kissed from him his passion. He could still see the whole length of it unspooling in the air between them, when she'd eaten it up like silver thread. Touching his lips, he wondered how he'd made it through the portal to begin with, and if he still needed the part she'd taken from him? But right now, he didn't have time to consider it. Callous was rising above the same rapids that had devoured Holly's rowboat and held him under. And then right there in the air, fifty feet above the spot where he died, a table came into view. The closer Callous rose, the more Holly could see chairs gathered behind it. *There were chairs in the air!* Then men appeared. Bigs and the other characters from the speakeasy in the Above sat watching as the mule and Holly floated up from the river.

"Callous?" Holly muttered, but the mule couldn't answer, couldn't stop churning his legs. From the frenzied charge of the beast, you'd have thought he was still in the rapids, thrashing against the driving current. "Where's Clevenger?" Holly said and watched the Potomac far below. It was a beautiful day. The sun shined as the mountains rippled with green and amber leaves and the breeze moved the treetops as birds drew black lines against the sky. Not much farther east a train whistle blared. "The 6 o'clock," Holly said. "In Brunswick. I hopped it many times on the way back from…" But he didn't want to name the card games he'd frequented. Or the all-nighters that kept him away from Nora. Silly games that lingered and moved whenever the police caught wind of them. Moving near the racetrack later in the evening usually, when a high roller from Atlantic City or Newark came through, and a high purse was attached to a horse.

"He'll wash up at Point of Rocks," Bigs said and turned in his chair. He looked with Holly at how the river cut its way through the Blue Ridge, carving its path. Another few miles after Brunswick was where Point of Rocks had the bigger rapids. The ones Holly hadn't even made it to that day fishing. *Why the hell had he taken a boat out anyway? Why wasn't wading good enough?* he wondered, as he looked at the fine suit Bigs wore. That they all wore. Silk jackets and shirts, perfectly tailored and creased, and he remembered he'd been trying to impress the friend he'd borrowed the boat from. Holly didn't want him to think he was wading in the muck for catfish, but searching the deeper spots for bass. "I have to say, Mr. Pride; I am impressed."

"It's just Holly. You can call me Holly."

"Of course. Holly. I can't recall anyone else ever making it back here—whatever the hell here is?" Bigs smiled and waved his hand at the cloud, and the boys surrounding him all chuckled and puffed their cigars.

"I died here."

"Oh, I know. We all go back to where we died; at least, the troubled dead do. And you, sir, are most definitely troubled."

"And dead," McCallan chimed in, to the general amusement of the others.

Callous snorted and Holly heard the mule's voice speaking to Bigs in his mind. It was clearer, the communication, and Callous must have been getting a bit more comfortable trotting for Holly to hear it. The mule wasn't thrashing as much, but had found a sweet spot in the eternal rhythm he was forced to tread.

I believe we're caught in an eddy, Callous said.

"A what?" Bigs said, and scowled at the mule.

A circular movement of wind, counter to the main current.

"Like a twister?" and Bigs held his hand out to feel the swirling breeze.

Someone else has forced this upon us.

Bigs stared at Callous, and the mule nodded his long head, and Holly watched Bigs react to the mule's movements. Bigs wasn't sure of the order here. Nobody was. If Bigs was in charge of his small portion in the Above, and Callous of his small portion in the Below, the two had never crossed paths before or purposes like this, and that was the way they'd always thought it would be. But either by the lazy murmur of the river far below, or the circumstance of working in tandem with the mule—Bigs was quiet. Reflective, even. "I just want to know why we're here. One minute we're all dancing, and the cabaret is jumping. Then it's like we've been sucked through a hole. And we're sitting above a goddamn river?"

Callous shook his mane and Bigs touched his temple, thinking. "Maybe," he said. "Maybe it is someone else. Another force altogether."

"A spell?" Holly said the word because Callous was thinking it and so was Bigs. "I saw a woman when we first came through. An herbalist."

"And you honestly think someone from down there in the living and breathing world could do this? That they could have the power to suspend your path and bring us all down here to decide on something? Impossible." Bigs leaned his hands on the table and only then realized he was standing in the air. Shaking his head, he wondered at the gaping disorder of the whole affair. Apparently, his reflective mood had soured.

"Wait—this isn't part of the procedure?" Holly said. "After I just got some of my parts back? I thought this was the next step!" Holly searched the eyes of all the men seated before him, twelve in total, and saw fear in each eye staring back.

"This, my friend, is some weird shit."

McCallan then climbed from his chair to the table and placed a hand on Bigs's shoulder, whispering in his ear. Holly remembered all the faces of all the men seated before him—the judges, or jury, he supposed—meant to decide whatever step was next. It was an excruciating feeling to think he was being judged. But at least they were confused about the same thing he was. At least, he had that working for him.

And their fear. Callous tilted his head, and the phrase popped into Holly's mind. But it wasn't just words. A deep, sonorous voice was attached to the words. *Don't underestimate the usefulness of their fear. And stop kicking me with your heels. You won't fall over.*

"Sorry."

"How's that?" Bigs had heard Holly speak once McCallan sat down.

"I said, 'Sorry to inconvenience you, but can we begin?'"

Good, press them. Make them rush into whatever it is they have to decide. Force them down a path they don't know, into a mistake, underplaying their hand.

Holly knew all about underplaying your hand. He'd seen it in any number of card games when a mark had a winning hand and thought he could pull out more dollars from the table. Betting piecemeal, teasing it all out, instead of going all in when it was obvious no one was falling for it. Too afraid to raise the stakes. Too afraid to win. It was the same with almost every person he'd ever met. Too afraid to take what was handed to them, whatever the advantage. His advantage was the fear of the situation, the uncertainty. And since he'd already somehow bested the butchering they thought Clevenger would administer, and had discovered the use of the object he'd found—the cup that had been the key to draining his way back into the living realm—he now had to scare them into releasing him for good. So he could die again. Or right whatever wrong he'd done by giving his parts away out of order. To hear the calling again. So he could rise into the Above the right way. Like maybe what Clevenger had just done, in dying to bring Holly to this place.

Callous nodded to hear it all tumble out in Holly's mind, for apparently there wasn't anything Holly could think that the mule couldn't hear. Not since the incidents of the last hour had bound them together.

"It's all I have, isn't it?"

"Excuse me?" Bigs heard Holly again and misunderstood. He didn't know the mule was intended to hear Holly's words, and Holly would remember not to speak out of turn again. He would think instead with what he needed the mule to hear.

"I meant, can we please get on with it?" and Holly crossed his arms. "You said so yourself. What the hell are we doing here?"

Bigs smiled. Maybe he'd just felt the pressure Holly was exerting, and knew that patience—deliberate and practiced patience—was his play. Let him twist. Let them both twist in the wind, literally. "Sure, sure, we can start. But first, we have to understand the charges. We have to know why we're here. And we have to review your file."

23

MISS MISERY HELD THE REINS AND DROVE MERCY down the dirt road to the highway. Nora had been so thoroughly exhausted by her work dressing Juney's grandmother, and then placing the woman into the coffin, that dragging the box outside—with Miss Misery's help—had taken all her last effort. Even lifting it as they had, an inch at a time, settling and then pushing it off a box they'd set in front of the cart, had happened as if in the periphery of her fatigue. Like a dream of muscle memory. A dream she was now forgetting as she slumped beside the coffin. The sky was magnificent. There were white puffs and a few high circling birds. The overwhelming blueness stretched up and as she looked into each blue pathway, she hoped Juney was safe somewhere—wherever it was. They hadn't told her even after she asked, but she suspected it was at the orphanage in Bolivar. Not far from the police station. Right up the road near the schoolhouse. But she'd promised Juney to bury the body as soon as she could, and so that was what she was doing. What *they* were doing.

She didn't know how Miss Misery had found her, or what she'd seen to bring her up that dirt road—with a cart, no less!—but she was grateful and touched her belly. *The bird's nest soup.* Maybe it did more than bring out feelings? Maybe it connected them in a way Nora didn't know? She did feel the woman knew her thoughts as if they were her own. That words weren't as necessary or pure. Not since the thoughts seemed to pass between them. Like, for instance, the burial. Miss Misery already knew the plot was bought. The cemetery wasn't far. She'd since taken the reins, let Nora lie there, and would lead Mercy along the road and then over the bridge into Harpers Ferry, before winding up through the cobbled streets. And Nora hadn't needed to say a word about any of it. Miss Misery just knew.

"Holly's eyes," Nora said and pointed at the blue sky. "It's just like Holly's eyes."

Miss Misery and Mercy paused. She hadn't heard anything from Nora the last half hour. Only the mule's pattering hooves had sounded with a slow cantering sway that shook through Miss Misery's arms and the cart. Of course, there were cars swooshing past and honking at them, but to hear Nora now was a relief. Something human rising above the day.

"I looked into them," Nora said. "Raised her eyelids to see him in her."

"And?"

"He was there. He stared right back at me. But they were dim. Like I'd never seen them in life. Or maybe like only after he'd had too much to drink, when he'd stumble in singing some song about starlight or stardust."

"Or moonlight?" Miss Misery smiled at the thought of it, but knew Nora wouldn't ever see Holly again, at least, not if she could help it. Oh, she'd smelled him certainly. After the man she'd met had left Nora's house. The man who'd come looking for the rowboat Holly borrowed. Miss Misery had explained it all, and the man had expressed his condolences, wondering why he hadn't heard about it yet, but he told her not to worry one second about the boat. To consider it a trifle when compared to the loss the house would have to confront. And as he turned to leave, his hat still in his hand, she'd touched his arm. As easy as that. She'd felt the passion she'd long suppressed, or hid. Or which the herbs and incantations had sucked dry from her over the years. It all returned in a bright wave. *Holly's passion.* The silver thread she'd spooled on her finger and eaten in front of him. His passion had surged out, and the man had turned to look at her and stepped right into her arms. "Just like that," she said and touched her lips, smiling.

"How's that?"

"I said, 'You saw him just like that, in her eyes.' Remarkable. Life, and what it brings us."

"It does bring us trouble, doesn't it?"

"And opportunity."

Nora was quiet then, considering what Miss Misery said, and Mercy snorted as a car went by and the bridge loomed closer, and Nora and Miss Misery could hear the rapids. The breeze blew a bit more briskly. High up, the church spire in Harpers Ferry loomed through the swaying leaves. A bell sounded six times. They'd make it up to the cemetery in another half hour. Just as dusk eased over the mountains.

"Remarkable," Miss Misery repeated, because she could still smell him. She looked from the bridge now that they were halfway across and down at the confluence—not two hundred yards away—a small misty cloud hung in the air above the rapids. A cloud that looked like it had descended from the ether to sit and visit with the valley and rivers below. The smell came from that cloud. *Holly's smell.*

She'd been down on the banks for an hour after that man left, the one asking about his boat. Francis was his name. Francis tall and eager, with a spark of mischief in his eyes. Or which the passion had brought out in him. And her. Yes—*mischief.* The word had her sitting cross-legged on the riverbanks. She was up to her own bit of mischief. The smell of Holly had absorbed her thoughts and feelings, but was a smell she wanted to push away. So he could never return to reclaim his passion. The possession she now held to her heart like one of her birds, her swiftlets. All the ones gone. The ones that had sustained her and her mother and her mother's mother before her. This passion was like that now. Sustaining, and Miss Misery remembered the distancing spell she'd recited. Sprinkling the burnt leaves of woad, the roots of silphium dipped in vinegar, and the crushed green glass of one of Holly's old whiskey bottles, sprinkling it into the air. She took it right from the doorsill that morning. Crushed it up in the yard, with some shards still scattered beneath the strawberry bush. He couldn't return if he tried. But still—*that cloud?*

"It's odd." Sitting up in the cart, Nora could see the cloud, almost as if she were listening to something her body needed. Something pushing her up to sit beside the coffin. "There's something above the rapids. Just hanging there. Do you see that cloud?"

Miss Misery looked a long time. They were almost across the bridge. They'd spill out into Harpers Ferry soon enough, and the trees and roofs and old buildings would block the cloud from view. Winding up into the ridge then, above the church to find the cemetery caretaker—the one to help them ease the coffin down with rope, till dusk fell, drawing its deep blue curtain across the night—would take time enough to obscure any cloud that might be calling to Nora. Calling with Holly's scent. Singing with his presence. "Cloud? Why, I don't see any cloud at all, dear."

24

EDISON APPEARED AND HOLLY'S CHEST HURT to see the man carrying a file—his file. Holly's wedding ring glistened on the man's finger. There was a power in seeing it on someone else. A power that had his chest pulsing and his brow breaking out in a raw sweat. The same ring she'd slipped on his finger the day they'd married at the Roanoke City Hall.

He hadn't even been able to give Nora a proper wedding. Just the two of them with the clerk witnessing as the judge invoked the "I dos" as they smiled and kissed. Holly bringing the rings out from his coat pocket (he'd won them in a craps game the night before, but hadn't told her). Nora as pretty as can be in a white sundress with orange trim and a bouquet of orange lilies. She'd traveled with him in a brand new 1926 Hudson sedan all the way down. He'd gotten a job delivering the automobile and held Nora in his arms that morning, still basking in the glow of asking her the night before if she wanted to get married. *Just like that.* He already had the hotel room rented in his name (as part of the layover for the job). They'd ride the train a better part of a day up through the Shenandoah Valley on the way back, and he'd considered it their honeymoon. He bought lemon ices from the food car as they'd sat by the window watching the world pass by. He hadn't even stopped to start a card game with a group of soldiers he'd seen in the bar car. Easy pickings. It was Nora's special day, and he held off. All he'd wanted was to sit by her, to smell her fresh smelling skin. The orange lilies. The honeysuckle smell of everything. Her hand in his forever.

"Three incidents, in particular, are what we're here to discuss." Edison pointed to the open file, eyed Holly with a sideways glace, before Bigs waved him back. Touching the ring with his other hand, Edison smiled at Holly, and was gone—evaporating into the misty cloud.

101

"I hate it when he does that." Bigs looked at the billowing cloud, turned to the other jury members, and looked at Holly. "You should have never given him that ring."

Holly remembered not having a choice. What did he know about bribery in the afterlife? "I thought it might help."

"They all think that." Bigs chuckled and tapped the file on the wide table. Below them, the rapids rushed with a constant pressure. Callous sighed and galloped slower, his chest frothing with sweat. Holly wasn't sure how much longer the mule could go like this and patted his neck.

"What three incidents are we here to discuss?" Holly recalled his only advantage might be to press the proceedings forward.

"We'll take them one at a time." McCallan said, and shifted in his chair. "The three incidents are the exemplars of your transgressions. Symbolizing the larger balance held against you. Everyone can boil their life's balance down to three incidents."

Holly couldn't think of anything held against him beside the body parts he'd given away and said so, but Bigs just shook his head.

"That behavior is peripheral. And I can understand how you might be confused, but it's inconsequential to the larger transgressions," McCallan added.

Holly had caught a whiff of something. An orange honeysuckle came to him in waves, and as he turned, he could see a mule cart lumbering off the bridge into Harpers Ferry. Then the trees blocked it from view, and all he had was the smell of her inside him—*Nora*. Wafting on the air to find him sequestered above the confluence, a judgement of his deeds held somewhere in the air around him, held in the minds of these men. A group he would have to confront and convince in turn. Convincing them that whatever he'd done wrong in the past was done for a reason.

"Nora," he muttered, and spotting the church spire, he wondered in his body how he could go there, too. His arms and legs wanted to hurl himself off Callous, but the mule could feel that and galloped higher—and the slight increase in the mule's height made Holly's thighs and heels clench tighter to the beast's body. *You're with me now*, Callous said in Holly's mind. *Just as Nora is with you. We're together, and I swear we'll find her after you answer for what you've done.*

"Yes, Nora does play her part in this." Bigs had heard Holly mention Nora's name and thumbed ahead a few pages. "Nora Grace, born March 15, 1904, in Bristol, Virginia. She's two years younger than you . . . and, oh my." Bigs had stopped short in reading anymore.

"What? What do you see?"

"All in due time, Holly. All in due time."

"You have no quarrel with her. I demand you leave her out of this."

"You're in no position to demand anything." Bigs stood and stalked the length of the table as the other men smiled and whispered, amused to hear Holly challenging Bigs—and them—by extension. Whatever position they found themselves in, as jury to his fate, they'd grown into the pleasure of it, and Holly's advantage of pressing them forward had dissolved.

"Just answer our questions and we'll decide. It's as simple as that. Somehow, you've gotten your eyes back. We can see that." Bigs pointed at the deep blue eyes Holly focused on them. "And we can see your chest is sewn up and that another heart beats inside."

"A bit too large, but a heart nonetheless," McCallan chimed in, tilting his large blonde head and listening to Holly's body. Blinking once, McCallan pointed at the misty cloud surrounding them, and Holly's beating heart began to pound as the anxiety of the situation fueled his adrenaline. Only Callous was able to ease him back, singing in Holly's mind an indeterminate tune with a tender feeling. That brought Holly's heart rate back to something more appropriate for a calm and rational man—exactly what he needed to be.

They're going to test you. They'll try anything they can, Callous warned.

I understand, Holly thought back. *I can do this.*

"Of course, there's still the matter of your passion. A part you can't find in any shape you might imagine it inhabits." McCallan had his own notebook in front of him, and ran his finger down a list of words that marked off the total loss of Holly's life. "By making it this far, I suppose you think you've already won something. A reprieve? Another chance to right your wrongs? To walk back to those riverbanks and see your wife. To tell her goodbye."

"I haven't won anything but your scorn, as far as I can tell."

Bigs smiled to feel the thrust of Holly's attack. If that was all the man had in him, it would go much quicker than he thought. Yawning at the melodrama of it all, he sat in his leather chair, and read again from the file. "The 1926 Hudson. Your drive down through Virginia. The hotel room and honeymoon and train ride back. Let's talk about that, shall we? About everything you took down into your body that wasn't yours to take?"

"What I took?"

"And about the life of Edward T. Flannery."

"Eddie T.?" Holly remembered his friend and long-time card player, and slumped atop Callous, bowing his head.

"Yes, let's talk about Eddie T., shall we? The man you killed."

25

NORA COULDN'T SEE THE CLOUD ONCE MERCY and the cart rattled down Shenandoah Street, spilling out at the bottom of Harpers Ferry. It was early evening, and a few people still strolled about. A bunch of folks from out of town lingered, too, swarming in packs on the roadside. They must have been in town for the re-enactment and might have thought the mule cart part of it, since the fake gunfight had just ended by the armory. Nora had seen this happen a few times before. She'd heard the musket shots and seen the puffs of smoke as they'd cleared the bridge, but it hadn't startled her. She didn't think at all about John Brown, about when he'd taken the town hostage and tried to lead his slave revolt all those years ago.

As Miss Misery drove, and some of the crowd pointed at the coffin and even applauded, Nora couldn't bother to see any of them. She was wondering about that cloud. Because she *had* seen it, no matter what Miss Misery said. Nora knew there was the scent of Holly in it. Something like sweet apple pie and horse leather. It carried in a breeze that ruffled the ends of her hair and the sleeves of her dress, and followed them up the street, climbing the ridge. Holly's presence seemed to intertwine its scent with the sound of Mercy's hooves clattering on the cobblestone. Nora reached out and she could feel him, hovering there with her. "*Holly,*" she whispered, and she swore Miss Misery's head tilted at the sound of her voice—and Nora wondered what the woman knew. If she saw anything about Holly in her visions? "How did you know to bring the cart to Juney's farmhouse again?"

Miss Misery had already answered this, but repeated what she'd said to comfort her. "I saw it, like I said. And I don't ask any more why they come to me, these visions. I just do whatever they tell me. The pictures said, '*Transportation*.' That you needed it and where you'd be. I saw the dirt road, the farmhouse, and knew where it was. I gather bergamot and hibiscus there all spring. It beamed into my mind as easy as that. I saw the empty cart in the yard next to the girl's house when I arrived and took it without asking." Miss Misery felt the unease circling behind her, and it wasn't just because people on the sidewalk were gaping to see a real-life funeral procession go by, or to know she might be accused of stealing the cart whenever she did bring it back. It was the scent. *That goddamn scent!* And Nora's reaction to it. Miss Misery knew it had lingered long enough. That the sweeping pulse of it had overtaken Nora's thoughts, and the only way to stave off any more complications was to head straight for it. To de-mystify it. Puncture its airy bloom and lightness, now that its influence invaded every inch of the space they occupied. "The scent of love lingers long, dear," Miss Misery said.

"So you smell it, too?"

"I've smelled it ever since he appeared in the woods. Ever since the scent brought me to him."

"Then did you see that cloud at the confluence?"

Mercy turned as Miss Misery pulled hard to the left, rolling up beside Saint Peter's Roman Catholic. "Did you know this was the only church in Harpers Ferry to escape destruction?"

Nora couldn't speak. Just burned to hear her admit it.

"During the Civil War, dear."

"And you're telling me this because..."

"Because it takes some doing not to go to hell when all else around you is doing just that. It takes some lighter touch and understanding to maneuver past any of the obstacles that have been placed before you. And I, well I'm like a guide for you now, against all those obstacles." The church sat on the left as they passed. A few last visitors wandered out, still held within the heady conviction of their prayers—and what met them, Nora wondered? Nothing but a cart of the dead. An omen of grief and stricture rummaging up the hill beside their lamentations of redemption and belief.

"*Jesus,*" Nora hissed. "You're really gonna sit there and tell me you didn't see that cloud because it might *help* me? That it was just some obstacle? And here we are, riding through town like some kind of harbinger for the dead. You don't think that's some kind of obstacle, too? Aren't we an obstacle to everyone else? Reminding them of each lonely end?"

Miss Misery gazed back at the awestruck churchgoers and chuckled. "They should be thanking us for what we're doing. We're giving meaning to their prayers. And even if you don't believe that, how about we look at it from the other perspective? What meaning do they have if they *don't* see us? Why pray to begin with? Why lament and struggle for redemption if not to see the death we all have it in us to become? Why go through all those motions, all those trials of belief and sacrifice if you're not reminded daily of where it all ends and why you need to believe in the first place?"

"Exactly. *I believe*. I believe I saw that cloud just now. I believe I smelled Holly's scent on me, on you, on Mercy—on everything. It's still here. *He's* still here. But for whatever reason, you think it's better for me to forget the man that gave you part of himself. A part I didn't have the occasion or grace to feel for many months before he passed. Many months." Nora was silent, thinking about Holly's passion for her and hers for him.

Holly had been distant for some time before he'd died. She'd been distant, too. Maybe the fact they couldn't conceive, couldn't bring life into this world, had taken its toll, when at first, they'd been as optimistic as they could about the circumstances. Nora had talked about adoption, fostering a child, about getting involved with the orphanage or schoolhouse, just to be around them. Children. And their energy. And Nora imagined the eerie spark that had danced between Holly and Miss Misery's lips, when they'd kissed on the ridge that whole lifetime ago. It seemed like a lifetime now, and she traced her lips and wondered about the bright passion Miss Misery had taken from him. The passion that was not hers to take, though she knew Holly had offered it freely. For apparently, that was what the dead did.

"I meant it when I said he had it in him, your man."

"To do what? To give me a child? So what. He's dead now. Or didn't you see that, too?" Nora slumped against the coffin. She had it in her mind to cry now for once; she realized she hadn't cried throughout this whole strange series of days. It was more like one long moment, this journey—that seemed to flash dark and then light and then dark again—and no matter how much she treaded through it, she didn't seem to move anywhere. Just treading time like treading water. Though she wouldn't give Miss Misery the satisfaction of seeing her cry. So instead, she just sat there. She sat and stared at the cloud, the one with Holly in it, as Miss Misery brought the cart and Mercy to a halt after climbing up amongst the headstones and gravesites.

Harper Cemetery stretched across a hill that overlooked the confluence and the town below. From there, they could see the upper tufts of the cloud that Miss Misery had lied about not being able to see. It wasn't completely covered by the trees as Miss Misery had hoped. It was still there, still visible, and as Miss Misery wondered about it, she could still smell Holly's presence wafting above the valley, surrounding them. And maybe she'd been wrong about this whole affair? Maybe the only way to keep her passion was to follow Nora's desire to find her husband? To somehow wrangle herself into that cloud, or to bring it crashing down to the rapids? So that Nora could see him. Or take any last bit of it that still lingered on his lips? Either way, it would take some doing, and as she thumbed through the invisible stores of herbs and tinctures in her mind, Nora stumbled from the cart and glared at her with her dark, angry eyes.

"Of course, I saw it," Miss Misery said, after she couldn't take any more of Nora's anger. Then she smiled easy as pie as the cemetery caretaker appeared, rope in hand. "I still see it. And I meant Holly *still* has it in him to give you that child. *Especially* since he's dead. Even if that might sound contradictory to you. But only if we help him, dear. Would you still like to help him?"

26

HOLLY SAT BEHIND THE WHEEL OF THE 1926 HUDSON and held Nora's hand. She was smiling and the sun had just set behind the racetrack as he headed for route US 11 and plunged the pedal down, the engine roaring as they rolled south. Roanoke was just a moment to him as he remembered it. But the moment stretched and resolved into shapes and scents and became a broad panorama that Callous and Bigs and all the jury members saw and experienced as he described it. The air itself had become a vast picture screen, but with depth to it and shape. And more than once as he spoke, Holly had to stop himself from reaching out and grabbing the stick shift, or steering wheel, or from patting Nora's rosy cheek. Nora. *Jesus*, she was right beside him, and she was eight years younger in her wedding dress, and he was in the nicest suit to this day he'd ever worn (the one he'd borrowed from Eddie T. after the last card game they played).

Eddie T.'s suit. Holly ran his fingers along the wide lapels. Down the smooth, creased length of the pants legs, the vest. The smoked ivory buttons. Even the wingtips were Eddie's, polished to a high sheen. Truth be told, Eddie had let Holly borrow the suit after Holly mentioned what he hoped to do now that he was driving the Hudson in Eddie's place. (Eddie, in another of his magnanimous displays that day, had passed a driving job off onto Holly as well.) The card game had gone on for much of the night and into the next morning, and the two other men who'd lasted long enough to see the sunrise saw another strange sight—Eddie T. stripping down to his underwear—and handing over his suit and shoes to Hollis Pride. What was surprising was that Eddie T. had been the big winner, and still he was the one handing over his suit. "Now to complete your look," Eddie T. said, before handing over a paisley pocket square, which he helped fold and shape in Holly's breast pocket, the car keys jangling in Holly's hands.

"To Roanoke? Tomorrow?" Holly remembered double- and triple-checking the destination, the instructions. Where to leave the car. How to place the keys in an envelope, address the envelope to Mr. Bowers, and place the envelope in the #16 luggage bin at the Roanoke Train Station. He then spent the better part of the next two hours arranging how to propose to Nora. Their neighbor, Mrs. Nuse from down the hill, said she could call Nora at the soda fountain and tell her to hurry home with a bottle of Dr. Guertin's Nerve Syrup for her boyfriend. She'd pretend Holly had taken a spill from the oak tree out back pruning it and had a spasm of some sort. Nothing too bad, but he might be in bed a day or two. A medicine show had just passed through town and set up shop outside the racetrack. If Nora hurried, she could find them on the outskirts of town. A bottle was $2, but Nora had the money, and Holly didn't feel the slightest shame in having her worry about him for a few hours. Mrs. Nuse, cupping her hand over the telephone as she said it, giggled and looked at Holly for any further instruction.

"Make sure she asks for tomorrow off," Holly said, straightening his tie after gathering the largest wildflower bouquet he could find. He was going to be in bed when Nora arrived, the covers pulled up to his chin. The bouquet was in a vase in the back seat of the Hudson. He would pull the covers back—yell *Surprise!*—and jump down to one knee with the wedding rings he'd won from Stackhouse Johnson (who himself had won them a week before from a desperate bridegroom). "The game hadn't been a total loss," he'd told Mrs. Nuse. "Even if I do have to drive to Roanoke with this car." Holly held up the rings, and pointed out front. The Hudson gleamed shiny and perfect, and he hoped Nora would think it was a doctor's car once she hurried home to find him sweaty and despondent, a wet washcloth on his head.

Bigs shook his head and reached up to touch the paisley pocket square. "You and Eddie T. were the same size, I take it?"

"Yes, sir."

"And did you ever give him back the suit?"

"No, sir. But I think you'll understand that once I finish."

Callous snorted and shook his head as Holly patted his neck. "I know it. I do." He *did* know what he was doing. He didn't have anything to worry about with Eddie T. He knew exactly why Eddie had died the way he did, and it didn't have anything to do with him. "In fact, I think you'll find my actions were in the right. That I only had Eddie T.'s best interests in mind."

There wasn't big money in that game, but it had been enough to move from hand to hand and cause them all to stay as long as they could to win the biggest share of it. Holly had just gotten paid from a job he'd done shingling a few houses in Charles Town, and Stackhouse, Eddie T., and Bishop had been burning to play for a week by then when the opportunity arrived. Bishop Reilly was someone to keep your eyes on during a game. Usually, Holly wouldn't sit down at a table with him if he was worried about losing, but he didn't feel any of those worries that night. He was buoyant. Joyous. He had the idea of asking for Nora's hand for some time and once he got to talking with Eddie and heard about the problem he was in—of driving the Hudson to Roanoke when he had another job lined up—well, it was all the opportunity Holly had hoped for. Putting that nugget of information in the back of his head, he let it sit there as the night wore on and the hands played out and the wins and losses piled up on all sides.

"You started giving away your hand about an hour ago," Eddie said and lit a cigarette; he passed it to Holly so he could share a puff. The game was done and the two of them watched the sunlight come up over the large grandstand. Holly had heard one of the sheds was being cleaned and the horses transported to Bluefield for the next two weeks. He'd gotten a table and a few chairs lined up straight away. There were a few colts on the track this early. Someone was up even before them, and from where they stood, they could hear the soft clay scattering beneath the hooves as the two horses were put through their paces.

"It was probably just fatigue, Eddie."

"Since when do you ever get tired?"

"Since I got other things on my mind." Holly then told him about Nora, showed him the rings he'd won from Stackhouse, the rings Eddie had forgotten about—since Holly had won them about six hours ago. Holly even mentioned maybe driving to Roanoke in Eddie's stead. "So you don't blow your other job, whatever that is."

"Yeah, my other job. I don't want to miss that." Eddie turned and patted Holly's shoulder and that was when they started disrobing right there in the doorway, as Stackhouse and Bishop shook the sleep from their eyes at the unordered turn of events—the winner giving the loser the clothes off his back. Eddie realized the moment and saw the utter disarray of Holly's attire and decided this one gesture was the best gift he could give to his friend on his wedding day.

"And?" McCallan stood and crossed his arms as Holly paused. Bowing his head, Callous knew inside the next words Holly would utter had brought a low feeling in the man's belly. Callous could feel it in his belly too, and jumped once to startle Holly back into coherence, to give him the courage to continue.

"And that was it. I never saw him again, except when the police brought me in to identify his body. The day *after* our train ride back from Roanoke."

"But you took his suit. You took his car," McCallan added. "You took his place. Taking, in essence, his life?" Bigs held a hand up as if to hush anything McCallan still had to say.

"Gluttony is what you're accused of, Holly. Of what you stole for yourself," and Bigs looked from the file to the man sitting atop the mule.

"I lost is what I did," Holly said.

"But it says right here you took from Eddie T., you took his place. His position. And he had to rob that store because of it. It just so happened his gun couldn't shoot."

Holly stared at Bigs and marveled at how even here, in a place between the living and dead—even here, folks couldn't listen and believe the truth. "I said he won that night. We all knew he was broke. Eddie T. was one of the biggest losers at the track. We let him win that night and spit and shook hands on it. Even Bishop came out on the losing end. We were trying to help."

Bigs scanned the file in front of him and shook his head.

"No matter what it says, I never took from him what he didn't give. I didn't know his other 'job' was a robbery, that the winnings we gifted him that night weren't enough. He wasn't a thief. Wasn't muscle either. He was just too confused and proud to ask for help. He was my friend, and if anyone killed him, it was because of the path he'd started down from the end of that card game to the front door of that soda fountain. The same soda fountain Nora worked in. It was just lucky we were already on the road. She never saw Eddie T. enter. Never saw the gun flash. Never heard the thunderous reply. Old Man Albert kept a shotgun on a shelf behind the counter and was a crack shot. If I'd known Eddie T. was gonna rob the fountain, I would have done anything I could to stop him. Honest. And if I couldn't, I'd at least have mentioned about Old Man Albert's shotgun. I would have helped."

27

THE NIGHT SWEPT OVER THEM AFTER THE LAST shovelful was patted down and the caretaker mumbled about how late it was before walking off. Mercy was eating grass and weeds growing from the other headstones, and Miss Misery was sitting cross-legged, mumbling over the grave when Nora felt a jolt. Something like a gun flash sounded in her mind, and she wondered if it was just remembered residue from the earlier musket blasts. The ones they'd heard the re-enactors firing off in their play war when they'd ridden over the bridge. Or if it was something else. Something deeper.

In her mind, she saw the 1926 Hudson that Holly had driven to Roanoke the day they married. Then the city hall in Roanoke that evening. Dusky light falling through the high windows in the rotunda. The last members of some elementary field trip had paused at the railing when Holly and Nora held hands saying their "I-dos." A hundred kids clapping and cheering for them. She felt the moment bubbling up inside her. The warmth of Holly's sweaty hand. His handsome suit—one she'd never seen before. The rings he'd surprised her with after that whole ridiculous ruse he'd concocted to have her take a day off, with Mrs. Nuse helping him, no less. Hurrying home that night, she'd thought Holly wasn't going to make it. She saw the Hudson in the yard and just knew it was some fancy doctor from Frederick or Baltimore. Because there he was sweating and writhing when she stooped over the blue bedspread, before smiling with that silly grin of his, standing up fully decked out in that suit. The Hudson smelled like a florist the whole way down with the bouquet wavering in the back seat.

"Mrs. Hollis Pride." She said the name and looked for that cloud above the confluence, and sure enough, a vague pocket of opaque color appeared. Like a glycerin bubble or soapy sphere. Something the wavering lights from town and the stars didn't reflect in. "Strange," she muttered and eyed Miss Misery who was done murmuring her spell, but who pulled a pinch of some brown spicy mixture from her bosom—from the tiniest cotton snuff bag she kept there—and sprinkled it in the air above the grave. Then leaning back, she clapped her hands as the cloudy mixture rose and fell in the breeze, spreading across the hillside until Mercy sneezed, breathing in some of the powder.

Almost at once Nora couldn't smell anything but cinnamon. She smelled black pepper and chalk, too, and remembered the soda fountain the day after marrying Holly. A man had tried to rob the fountain. It was the end of August and Old Man Albert kept the money for the month's deposit behind the counter underneath his shotgun in a metal cash box. Everyone in town knew it, but there wasn't much robbery—let alone *armed* robbery—in Charles Town. The racetrack gobbled up most of the unsavory activity. So it was a cold awkward store she walked into that day. Old Man Albert stepped back from his duties after the shock of it all, of taking a man's life. It hadn't been as easy as it first seemed. Especially after the police said the man's gun could barely shoot, and if it did, it couldn't have shot straight in the least. They lost a lot of regular customers after that. Folks didn't want to buy ice cream for their kids and root beer floats in an establishment where a killing had taken place. Nora remembered one customer though. A woman. Tall and scraggly. Her hair a ruined weave of sticky strands and knotted clumps. The woman never looked up from the old notebook she brought. Never stirred much either aside from mumbling to herself. Nora could never tell if the woman actually was reading from it or if it was more a focus for her harried gaze. As if she were absorbing whatever information was there rather than offering any. But Nora brought the teapot the woman always ordered and never knew why she'd been so haggard and sad until now.

"Eddie T. Flannery." Nora hadn't said the name since she'd read it in the *Fredrick Post* all those years ago, which reported on the shooting like it was the biggest thing to hit the area since the Spanish Flu. She only found out later from Hollis it was one of his gambling buddies.

Miss Misery stood from the dead woman's grave and shook her legs out, before bowing to the headstone. It was as if she was even then seeing the raised spirit. Maybe they'd been speaking all that time? The thought of it sent shivers down Nora's spine.

"It was you." As Miss Misery came closer, Nora watched her wipe the tears from her cheeks, before she smiled thinking of her long-dead boyfriend.

"Eddie was so stupid." Miss Misery laughed, thinking of him. "I can't believe you said his name. How'd you know?"

Nora pointed at the eerie soap bubble hanging above the confluence. "Something is happening in there, and these memories that I have with Holly are coming out—they're making connections. I had no idea you were with Eddie."

"Nobody did. We kept it secret. He was always worried about appearances. Just like he always thought he'd hit it big on a horse one day. That was his dream. He'd make a few dollars at a job during the week, selling shoes door to door, or driving around cars. Then he'd go blow it all at the track, but win just enough at poker or craps to think he was somebody on the make. Somebody who was gonna *be* somebody. I still can't believe I liked somebody like him. Like you, I guess."

Nora felt Miss Misery's eyes pouring into her and wasn't sure what she meant.

"Someone with a regular job, is all I mean. With a home, and bills to pay, appearances to keep. Someone tied into whatever this world thinks we should be doing to keep it going. We were always the odd ones. The fortune-tellers, the drifters. Like carny folk, I suppose. On the outside looking in. Maybe that's why I liked him so much. He was fun to watch. He struggled so damn hard to be regular, when I couldn't care less about it. I still don't."

"But you must've cared. I saw you back then at the fountain with your ragged hair. Your eyes. The notebook you couldn't stop searching for answers in. I didn't know who you were, but I could feel your pain. Like now, in just saying his name."

Miss Misery traced her lips and knew Nora was right. She hadn't wanted any man since Eddie died, and that was eight years ago. For eight years, she tried to hide the fact. She went about the business of trying every spell and tincture she'd ever learned from her mother. All the swiftlets she kept and cared for. Making sure the birds were comfortable, taking care of their nests, before making the soup from them—the big-ticket item. Telling fortunes, reading palms, selling tinctures for heartache and tuberculosis was nothing compared to the money from the soup. But when she smelled the dead man that day, Holly's smell rising through the woods, she realized she hadn't thought about Eddie in all that time. She'd blocked him out and everything he stood for. *Her heart.* She'd tucked it into the darkest corner. But there it was again on Holly's lips, as she spooled off his passion, and she didn't even know why she'd done it to begin with. Maybe it was just to make it to this moment. "To remember," she said, and held her hand to her heart. "You've allowed me to remember him."

"I think Holly did." Nora pointed at the bubble above the confluence, and the cinnamon scent Miss Misery crafted with her mixture had dispersed. Holly's smell returned as another breeze picked up, and Mercy's ears trembled because the mule was shivering at something else Miss Misery had forgotten to tell Nora.

"Ester knows all about it."

"Who?"

"Juney's grandmother, the woman we just buried. She was so happy we placed her beside her husband. With Holly's eyes, she could see her love again, and knew she could rise now. Knew a voice was trembling somewhere for her to hear. Some sort of calling, she said. Something they all hear, the dead, in their own way. Well, she told me Eddie was alright with everything. Knew he'd ruined things between us. And he's sorry." Miss Misery took Nora's hand, and Nora could see Ester atop her gravestone, glittering and grinning to see them watching. She was an ethereal blue and wavered like a bedsheet hung on the line. Only a second was what Nora was given. A second of the woman grinning and touching her heart before a current brushed her away, and when Nora looked again there were nothing but stars above the hill. Mercy was already moving. Miss Misery had turned the cart around. "Well, are you coming?"

"Where?"

"For Juney, of course. Ester knows where she is. She just told me."

28

HOLLY SAT ATOP JOSIAH PAUL'S HOUSE on the South Mountain Ridge near the Weverton Cliffs, almost five miles below Harpers Ferry with a hammer in his hand and a dozen nails sticking out of his mouth. He was younger. Stronger. He sat atop the house in the morning and saw the mist rising from the green treetops and breathed the fresh morning air. Josiah's pretty wife Marlene was brewing coffee and cooking eggs, and Holly usually arrived early on jobs like this so he could get fed a hearty breakfast after he'd already spent an hour ripping up rotten shingles. His stomach was already rumbling when he heard Josiah working on his front porch with a small hand drill. He had sandpaper and glue as well.

It was easy to see Josiah from where Holly sat, and he didn't feel in his body that Josiah wanted to be seen or called down to, so Holly kept hammering in the nails and slapping down shingles as he watched Josiah's peculiar movements. He was working on something small. It was so small Holly had to lean over the edge of the roof once he'd made it near the rainspout. The house was shaped like an L, and Holly, from his far position at the top of the L, could see Josiah in his position, at the bottom of the L. He sat and kept shaking something in his hands before tossing it on a picnic table. After he was satisfied doing this routine a few minutes, he raised his arm to look at the morning light through a glass vial of silvery liquid. It was a substance not unlike the one Holly had seen unspool from his lips, when Misericordia had kissed him and gobbled up most of his passion. Holly's mind flashed to the memory of it and for an instant, seated atop the house, he could see himself seated atop Callous, and he shook his head to bring back the vision projected around him of the hills and sky and silvery vial. "*Mercury?*" Holly said, and his questioning voice must have projected much louder in the mountain air, considering Josiah smiled and pointed for him to come and join him.

118

"Coffee?" From a steaming metal pot, Josiah poured Holly a cup. The mercury vial sat in the middle of the table, and as Holly eyed it, Marlene brought out scrambled eggs, bacon, and buttered toast and then left the men to whatever it was they were up to. Holly could sense the unease in her. Could feel it rising up to the cloud above the confluence. His younger self hadn't the slightest notion about the woman and her desire for stability. Especially not from whatever scheme Josiah was working on. Imagine, a man with all that talent—his woodworking and carving mastery—how it made him a commodity in the hills. He could have good paying work lined up for months, but instead chose these pet projects Marlene couldn't believe for the frivolousness of them. They were fantasies, really. Grifts. Confidence schemes, as far as she could tell. As if every man that grew up in the hills had it in his mind to risk it all on one big strike. Of course, all Holly saw back then was Marlene wiping her hands on her apron as she disappeared inside. There was no undercurrent of distrust. No misgivings or worry. Instead, he'd leaned in once Josiah—obviously enamored with his own craftsmanship—laid it all out for the young roofer.

"You're right. It's mercury." He held up the vial, and they watched the liquid tumble in its cloying way from end to end. "And look at these." Josiah swept his arm back, and Holly saw what the man had been working on. There were three pair of dice on the table. Two sets were already complete, while the third had been cut diagonally, so that the middle of each tiny cube was exposed. In the dug-out interior, Josiah had set a hardened wax ball. He was now working on a cross-section of a dumbbell-shaped insert. It was the smallest hollow wooden piece Holly had ever seen. But with the man's ability, he'd shaped it as few could, and was now raising a small spout he'd twisted from parchment paper. "Hold this here." He pointed for Holly to hold the top of the paper spout. Then Holly watched as Josiah poured from the vial the smallest drop of mercury. It slithered from the spout to the bottom of the dumbbell, which acted like a reservoir. With glue, he attached the other lengthwise half of the dumbbell, pressed it tight—before sealing it with a lit match. "Now I just have to place this inside." He situated the dumbbell in the wax, with the top in the middle and the end pointing to the number six. He'd already done the same in the other die, except the end of the dumbbell pointed toward the number one. He then glued the halves together.

"They're tappers?" Holly said, and he wasn't sure where he'd heard it, but Josiah looked him up and down and smiled.

"I didn't know you knew anything about loaded dice?"

"Read about it once in a comic book."

"Well, here's the rub," and Josiah pointed at the dice. "Each set comes up with a different 7. That first one lands 4 and 3, the second 5 and 2, and the third 6 and 1. See the trick is," and he held a pair up so Holly could see. "The trick is to palm the other sets. So when someone's suspicious," and as he rolled the first pair a 4 and 3 appeared right as rain, "when someone's suspicious, I pick them up and you shouldn't even notice. Even sitting beside me." Josiah grabbed the dice, closed them in his hand, shook them, and with his next roll a 5 and 2 came up.

"Hot damn!" Holly couldn't help himself, but grabbed Josiah's arm, and as the man opened his hand, the second set of dice tumbled out. Holly could see down the man's sleeve. He had the third set just inside his wrist. They were held there by a thick rubber band. All he had to do was reach down with his fingers and pull them up.

"Of course, when I change the one from my cuff, I have to drop the original pair down my shirt. That's where it gets tricky. I've got a sticky pad wrapped on my elbow to catch them. But to do that, I need a distraction." Josiah pointed at Holly.

"Me?"

"You seem interested. Do you want to be my distraction tonight?"

HOLLY AND JOSIAH HAD BEEN GOING NONSTOP to the smaller run-of-the-mill games for three months by the time Mr. Gettys's game rounded into view. It was not a moving game, nothing so pedestrian. Meaning Mr. Gettys had the Charles Town police in his pocket. He didn't have to run or get antsy when every other craps game had to have lookouts and an exit strategy and other locations to move to week to week, staying one step ahead of the law. Mr. Gettys was tall and lean, and some said he'd been a bootlegger from Boston or Miami. No one could place his accent. Somehow, he'd ended up here though, by the racetrack, and maybe even had a stake in it, since he was on such good terms with every owner in the shed row. Most of the trainers sat in on a game, and when Holly and Josiah arrived, Holly recognized three men straight off. He'd done stable work for them some months back, but he didn't expect them to remember, and anyway, the whiskey was flowing, and every eye was on Mr. Gettys. He sat on a stool at the end of the bar every night, closest to the table, swirled his whiskey, and watched the action unfold.

"It ain't any different here. Just set up like we always do and watch my lead. We don't want to win too much this first time." Josiah nodded to Holly and then turned to the room. Holly's play was to get a drink. Down it in a quick jolt, making a bit of a scene. He'd pound the bar, demanding a second—then bolt that shot, too. By the third drink, folks were usually smiling and patting him on the back, saying stuff like "Tough day?" Or "Slow down, fella. You got all night." And that was what he wanted. He was a character in their minds. No one to worry about, just more amusement. When Josiah was on a streak, Holly would stumble a bit closer to the table, and just by approaching, most folks looked at him, and it was enough for Josiah's first switch. Josiah would lose then on his next throw using the table's dice, and no one was any wiser. By the time his turn came around again, Josiah was ready, and they made out that first night with $200. Split it right down the middle, and that was why Holly kept coming back. Josiah understood Holly held as much risk as he did. They were partners.

"No way I've never seen this before." A waitress had sidled up to Holly the third night they visited Mr. Gettys's game. Holly had already had his three drinks, and even stamped his feet a bit in a sort of clogging dance to freshen up his routine, when she touched his shoulder. "He wants to see you."

"See me? I'm right here, darling. Anyone can look!" Holly took a bow before the waitress and was only doing it to bide his time. Leaning into his drunkenness was his only play, and he could feel the sweat standing out on his brow to know Mr. Gettys was wise to something. But it was best to play the dumb drunk all the way though, he figured.

"You're enjoying yourself, I hope." Mr. Gettys never stopped watching the game as he spoke, but Holly didn't turn from him. Couldn't. There was some darker magnetism happening here. Some deeper draw.

"I am, sir. Most deeply," and Holly bowed in his clownish way and even threw in a hiccup for good measure.

"Please. You two have quite the racket. I'd say tappers and a few pair. It's good. Haven't seen anything as smooth in some time. You're the distraction. Obviously." It was the only time he turned from the game to look into Holly's frantic eyes.

"Sir, I'm not sure I understand what you..."

"Save it. He changes dice whenever you do something to draw attention. Just a moment. It doesn't have to be big. But you're good and he's good and I want to offer you something, Hollis Pride. Something I think you'll enjoy just as much."

He knew Hollis's name. Holly turned to catch Josiah's attention, but Josiah was deep in a run. He was winning too much this time. Holly couldn't trip or spill a drink or do anything to get away from the gravity that Mr. Gettys cast upon him.

"The track and I have a . . . certain relationship, you might say. You might also say I've seen you working now and then in the stables. Saw you ride one morning, too, when that Delaware jockey was hurt. You filled in during the morning routine and weren't half bad."

"Sir?"

"I could place you in a stable as a jockey. As easy as that. All I want for you to do, is a switch; I want to see it. I want you to stand beside your partner Mr. Paul there, tap him on the shoulder, pick up his dice and replace them with these."

"He had a pair of dice in his palm. Holding them out, it was my body that grabbed them. My body that wanted to ride that horse. My body that wanted to race so badly, nothing else mattered. But my mind. Well, my mind had other designs."

Callous snorted and Bigs and McCallan and the jury seemed held in a state themselves, drawn in by each word. Much like how Holly had been drawn to Mr. Gettys—and Holly wondered if Mr. Gettys had a reputation here as well?

"Josiah didn't know Mr. Gettys had seen through our act. The third visit was when Josiah wanted to make his killing, making at least a grand before leaving. He didn't expect we'd come back for at least six months. When we'd start it all over. The three-night cycle was what we called it. Well, I tapped his shoulder as Mr. Gettys instructed. Told him I wanted to try, and he looked at me and just knew it was over. But smiling, he played it cool and watched as they all did, as I leaned over the rail. Cupping the dice as effortlessly as I could, I handed the new set to him. Like I was his good luck charm or something. Of course everyone eyed me for the etiquette I'd just broken, touching another man's dice during his run, but Mr. Gettys must have nodded to the room, because no one said a word. Josiah just shook the dice and laughed. He'd gone all in on this one and didn't even look once he rolled. Not even when the table erupted as the dice tumbled to their conclusion. We were already headed for the door by the time Mr. Gettys's men escorted us behind the bar to another room. Back to another table, where there was only Mr. Gettys to play. Josiah had won. He'd won it all. He'd hit a seven on the last roll I think he ever threw."

29

MISS MISERY BROUGHT MERCY AND NORA and the cart to rest outside the Bolivar Home for Wayward Youth. It was a large, towering building with three floors of gray windows and chipped brick chimneys. There were more wayward youth than you could imagine near Harpers Ferry. The Great Depression had cast so many able-bodied men and women out to find work, sending them across whole states and continents to find it. Some sent back money. Some disappeared forever, and some kids just got lost in the mix. And for whatever reason, the Bolivar home was the only one this side of Frederick with any reputation for actually doing what the state mandated. Providing safety and comfort. Food and mentorship. Even some schooling and job training for the older kids—if they didn't manage to run away before all that training got through with them first. But Miss Misery wasn't thinking about any of that. Nora looked and Miss Misery's face was lit from within by her passion. It raced from her mouth up her cheeks, before shooting out in silvery sparks from the tips of her hair.

"I'm afraid I'm a bit unstoppable right now," she said, and Nora had to shield her eyes. Even Mercy snorted to see the pulsing warmth in the woman. She seemed possessed by an otherworldly glow, something kindled and growing. As the spirits of love and desire and compassion in this effort to get Juney back surged through her, she glided from the cart to the front door. Nora looked once at Mercy—who shook her head in a way that seemed to imply *anything* might happen here—which Nora agreed with, before hurrying after.

"Hello? Hello?" Miss Misery knocked and then tilted her head as inside she heard footsteps that sounded as if they were never getting any closer to the door.

"Do you have a plan?" Nora stood beside her and still gaped to see the silvery glow saturating the air surrounding her.

"Hope a man answers?" Miss Misery turned to Nora as the door swung open and a medium-sized gentleman with glasses and a beard stood there; his arms were crossed, and a napkin was tucked into the top of his collared shirt. "Bingo."

MISTER ANDREW EVANS WAS NOT WHAT NORA would have considered a romantic. But for the better part of the last thirty minutes—as he stammered at Miss Misery and shuffled from his front desk to the two chairs where he'd insisted they sit, bringing them tea and sugar cookies that the children had baked that evening—he couldn't stop staring at her. Couldn't pretend to do anything else.

"This is a most remarkable circumstance, you must admit." Nora tried again telling her story about losing Juney in a cave. That the girl had been despondent about the recent loss of her grandmother and had wandered off in search of some flowers to place at her gravesite, when she'd headed off unbeknownst into the dark.

"Well, the police don't seem to think so."

"*The police.*" Miss Misery just had to speak, and Andrew fell silent. "What do they know?" He swayed behind his desk. He hadn't been able to sit the whole time they'd been trying to get upstairs to find Juney. A big double-wide staircase ran up into the depths of the house behind him. He would gesture back without looking whenever he mentioned the children. As if they were some resource he could dip into and out of, settling them back on their shelves once he was through.

"The police don't want her disturbed until the social services counselor comes tomorrow afternoon."

Nora was quiet, looked at the man, before sipping the last of her tea. "Sir, I'm not sure if you know this, but Juney has had a rough few days. And we're just here to give her a warm, comfortable place to stay until her meeting with social services tomorrow."

"Oh, *bullshit.*" Miss Misery scowled at Nora and dropped her teacup rattling to the saucer.

"Excuse me?" Andrew had to slap himself twice to stop staring at Miss Misery to understand what she was saying.

"We're here to take her home, and that's that."

"Take her home—*for the night*," Nora corrected and raised her eyebrows as if speaking in code to Miss Misery.

"You don't have to worry about any of that. Jesus." Standing, Miss Misery sauntered toward Andrew, and the man blushed from head to toe the closer she came. "I should've done this the moment we came in. Then we wouldn't have had to drink that awful tea." Touching Andrew's arm, Miss Misery flared silver and luminescent. As she leaned closer, he blinked and smiled in a stupor, love-struck by it all. "Won't you be a good dear and tell us what room she's in?"

"*Is he okay?* We haven't harmed him, have we?" Nora was at the bottom of the stairs and watched as Andrew teetered in Miss Misery's arms. She wasn't hurting him, Nora could tell. Just holding him up. It seemed he might fall any moment to feel her touch melt so deeply into his life.

"*Andrew?*" A knock at the door had Nora skittering upstairs. Miss Misery saw Sheriff Bay trying to look in through the curtained window. "Everything alright in there? I saw the mule cart. Folks said it took a coffin through town earlier tonight."

"Christ, am I going to have to touch him, too?" As Miss Misery watched Nora's scurrying feet disappear into the depths of the house, the sheriff opened the door. The only thing she could think to do was grab Andrew by the ankle and crouch behind him. As long as she kept hold of him and breathed a hot breath on his flesh, they might make it through this. She could give Nora time to find Juney. *But then what?*

A shriek in the upper room answered her question. The sheriff pointed at Andrew, but Andrew couldn't speak. He just shrugged his shoulders as Miss Misery sprang up from her spot. As the sheriff reached for his gun, shocked to see a silver vision appear, Nora came bursting down the stairs, a piece of paper in her hand.

"Mame?" The sheriff turned and pointed his gun at Nora, losing sight of Miss Misery, who'd already let go of Andrew and lunged at the sheriff.

"Her room. On her bed. I saw it. She's gone. The note. *The note!*" As she ran past the desk, Nora waved the paper in her hand.

"Well, what's it say?" Miss Misery had ahold of the sheriff and must have traced a finger along his neck, because the man was a quivering pudding cup. All his strength and determination were gone. He swayed standing there and couldn't speak, but watched helplessly as Nora raced out into the night. All as Miss Misery leaned in for a deep, smoldering kiss.

30

"WAIT, I DON'T UNDERSTAND." BIGS STOOD and shook Holly's file as several other men banged the table to hear the rest of the tale of Mr. Gettys and Josiah Paul. "None of this makes any sense. It says right here you *did* change the loaded dice. That you *did* exactly what Mr. Gettys demanded—you gave Josiah the dice Mr. Gettys wanted him to use. By even touching them, you betrayed him, destroying your partnership. Afterward, he fell into disrepute. Was branded a cheat. A liar. Wasn't allowed to gamble anywhere in town, and ended up drinking himself into a stupor."

"Ended up on the railroad." McCallan added and shook his head. "Sprawled across the tracks. And you know how that ends."

"Even Marlene couldn't go on. Started walking the streets of Frederick after they lost their house. Disgraced. Alone. Your greed set all that in motion," Bigs said. "He not only drank himself to death, but you sent his wife out to her cruel fate. *You* did that—by wanting more for yourself."

Holly shook his head at all of it, even as Callous whinnied to hear the pain inside the man in reliving each broken memory. "There's so much more you don't have. There's so much unwritten in those files."

Holly then described the room where Mr. Gettys waited for them behind the bar. The low chandeliers. The plush green table. "It's brand new. Something we've just created." Mr. Gettys purred and gestured for Holly and Josiah to come closer. Mr. Gettys's bodyguard had relaxed his grip from their arms, and as they stepped to the table, Holly felt again the gravity of the man. The pull of Mr. Gettys's personality, his position—it enchanted him. Josiah, on the other hand, was sweating. Beads of it lined his brow. He'd fumbled all their winnings into his pockets once they'd been found out, and $10-bills spilled from all parts of the man the closer he leaned over the rail to touch the felt table.

"How much do we owe you? I can get it, and we'll be on our way." Patting his pockets, Josiah didn't want to look into Mr. Gettys's eyes. No one indebted to him ever did.

"I'd say it's a bit more than what you made off with." He pointed at the bills spilling from Josiah's hands and pockets. "But it's bigger than that. You two set a precedent that others out there might find instructive. They might think they too could devise a plan to cheat Mr. Gettys out of his own money. *In his own establishment.*" Mr. Gettys tumbled the ice in his drink. He nodded to a man in a corner and a whiskey bottle was brought and his drink refreshed. "I'm guessing three different sets of dice. All loaded with mercury. You change them whenever the clown gets sloppy enough to divert attention." Holly blushed to hear himself described in such discarded terms. He didn't know if Mr. Gettys was going to tell Josiah about their arrangement. Even though, after all of it—after the offer of the horse, of being placed as a jockey in a stable and everything—he hadn't done it. He hadn't been able to change the dice, double-crossing Josiah, and he wondered if Mr. Gettys knew.

"We never tried to take too much," Josiah added.

"Maybe that was why I noticed? It was winning too little the first and second time that caught my attention. I figured there was too much control, restraint. If it was an actual true winning streak—a natural run against the odds—it would be boundless, lasting a bit longer. But yours . . . almost followed a schedule."

Josiah shook his head to see where they'd been wrong. It was their cautious, incremental approach that had given them away.

"But what I'm more interested in now is Mr. Pride's decision."

Shit. Holly bowed his head. He could feel Josiah looking at him. A burning pain pulsed in the center of his heart. It throbbed as if he'd been shot with a fiery bullet. He was going to tell Josiah about the arrangement—*he had to*—as the sound of horses thundered in Holly's heart, running away. "He asked me to change the dice on you." Holly blurted it out before even looking up. Before even sensing Mr. Gettys had motioned for two more glasses to be brought, and whiskey poured all around.

"So that's why you came to the rail?" Josiah shook his head and Holly looked, but Josiah just swirled the ice in his own glass.

"But after all that, I didn't do it. I couldn't. I gave you back the same pair you were using. He let us roll your own loaded dice."

Mr. Gettys smiled at the realization. "I figured as much," he said and chuckled. "At least, you've still got your *pride*, Hollis," and he nodded for them to watch as he placed $2,000 on the table. "I'll even let you use your dice on this throw. All you have to do is match my bet."

Josiah looked at Holly, and the old spark flashed in his eyes. It'd been gone since they'd been found out, and Holly shook his head, thereby telling Josiah by no uncertain terms was he to try and throw dice here. That he was sorry he'd even entertained the idea of cheating him. But he hadn't cheated him. He hadn't. But whatever Mr. Gettys had planned now for them, they could still find another option. They could place all their winnings on the table, place their watches too, and whatever else they had in their pockets to make up for the other two nights, and just leave and never come back. Holly said all this with a look and Josiah chuckled to hear it when there was such a sucker bet right in front of them.

"My own dice, you say? The ones I just won with?"

"All you have to do is match me." Mr. Gettys leaned closer and tumbled his thumbs over the whiskey glass. "Or didn't you get enough from me out there?"

Josiah was pulling bills from every part of his suit and stacking them on the table, counting as he went. He got to $1,000 and patted his empty pockets, placed his watch on the pile of bills and nodded at Holly, who placed his watch on as well.

"I'd say you're still $750 short . . . if I'm being generous." Mr. Gettys looked as if he were sniffing some foul air when he inspected their watches, before placing them back on Josiah's pile.

"My house!" Josiah had a pen and was writing it on a napkin. "Here's my word passing over the deed. But if I do this, you need to add another five hundred."

"Done."

As Mr. Gettys slapped another $500 down, Holly felt his feet burning. He'd already been shot in the heart with the shame he felt for even considering cheating Josiah, but now his body knew this man wouldn't let them use their own crooked dice unless he was certain they'd lose. Holly wanted to grab Josiah's arm, to grab the napkin he'd written his deed on and run. His feet were telling him to run, but something stopped him. Josiah looked at Holly and opened his palm, and the dice sat as inconspicuous as ever. Tapping them on the rail, Josiah had shifted the mercury down through the dumbbell to rest on the bottom of the dice. A 4 and 3 would surely show once they stopped tumbling, and without hesitation Josiah threw, and Holly felt all the air leave him. Mr. Gettys sat as still as a statue. He didn't even watch. Already knew the outcome. He had his foot on a switch that activated a vibrating coil rigged to the underside of the table. The vibrations—which couldn't be seen in the smooth felt surface, or heard even the tiniest bit in the room—sent a disordered chaos out through the liquid mercury, and the smile on Josiah's face melted away as snake eyes stared back at him.

"Just like they used to use in the Old West," Bigs said, and shuffled behind his chair. As Holly looked, the memory of it all snapped off, and the mountains and night sky came tumbling back.

"I'd never heard of it before. Josiah neither. But Mr. Gettys scooped up his winnings as if it was all another game to him. One he'd played for ages. One he never lost. I never did see Josiah again after that night. There wasn't any use telling him I was sorry. We'd been beaten by a better grift. One Mr. Gettys had just been waiting to play. But why wasn't all that in there?"

Bigs shook the file, sat back down, stood again and scowled at Holly before sneering at Callous for good measure. "I'm not sure. But I suppose we can find out. There's an object you left here, something from your life. Something with the last traces of your truth—whatever that truth might be."

Holly knew exactly what he meant and touched his finger out of habit.

"That's right," Bigs said, smiling. "You gave Edison your wedding ring. We'll just have to see what the ring has to say about all this."

"What the ring has to say?"

"Well, sure. You don't think we're the only ones who can talk and feel and remember? We'll send for him at once. Edison!" he called and crossed his arms. "Though as we wait—for I'm sure he knows why I'm calling and will take as long as possible to appear—you can tell us about the third incident."

"There is no third incident."

"You've already killed a man," McCallan said, his voice rising across the table. "You've already sent another man out to die, his wife into a life of abuse and neglect. Now tell us about the child. The one you wouldn't help bring into this world."

31

JUNEY HAD WRITTEN ONLY A SINGLE LINE on the paper Nora found. But Juney must have felt something deep inside that told her Nora would be the one to find it, considering she'd written something only Nora could have known:

Where I tugged on his hand.

Nora repeated the phrase as the cart rattled beneath them. They'd made it to the bridge, and it was somewhere past midnight, but still a few lights in Harpers Ferry were lit, and the glassy sphere above the confluence hung as they'd seen it before. But this time when Nora looked, she felt as if something was leaving her. As if all the effort she'd made in the world to love Holly was flowing away. Like so many coins falling in a well. It sounded like coins echoing on a sidewalk. She turned to Miss Misery to see if she heard it, too, but the woman just held up her hand as if to shush Nora from saying anything. There was something she was listening to behind all that coin-rattling noise. *Maybe it was a pathway?* A line of communication into the cloud? Or at least an inkling to what spell she would need to bring that cloud crashing down to the rapids. Nora wanted to go out there. To be beneath it when somehow Miss Misery brought it down. But first they needed to find Juney. *And a boat!* And maybe a stiff drink. Because it was getting harder to understand where all this was headed. Whiskey would be good, and as she thought about it, the scent of a neat glassful of Holly's favorite spirit wafted up over the bridge, and Nora got heady just sensing it.

"And horse leather, of course," she said, because those were Holly's smells to her. In the same instant, she smelled the racetrack. Its odor came drifting in behind the whiskey scent, and she pointed her nose at that hovering cloud. It was listening to her. Or responding to her thoughts. As if a parallel conduit raced from her to it and back again.

"We'll need extract of henbane to amplify the love between you two. Anise oil for protection and foreseeing. I have vines from the deepest thicket in the ridge. I left them to dry on a blanket lined with amaranth leaves. For invisibility. We'll need to match invisibility for invisibility. Kind for kind and like for like."

Nora was dumbstruck by the list. Miss Misery rattled off more names and herbs and extracts as she rumbled the cart and Mercy onto the side of the road once they'd made it across the bridge.

"Of course, you'll have to find a boat and some oars. We'll need to stay steady beneath the cloud if we're to have any hope of breaching its magnetic sphere. *Lodestone dust—of course!* I have it in a sack beside the cistern and the copper pipes in the basement."

Mercy sighed to hear the litany of items she would have to haul up and down the roadway for however long it took, but bowed her head regardless. There was some hypnotic current in the air. Some unseen force was moving Miss Misery onto a course she should've been considering all along. Long before she'd sat on the riverside and cast that spell up to send Holly away, keeping all his passion for herself. That was before she'd figured helping him might be better. Might send him off forever. For whatever trial he was going through—which most certainly had to do with the parts he'd handed out—had kept him hovering this close to the world of the living. But it all might be ended if she helped him. He might not even need his passion back, if he had his heart and eyes? Maybe she hadn't even taken all of it from him? Or he might only be inclined to take back half, if she helped. If the binding spell worked. Binding him again to Nora. She'd have to see.

"We'll need to split up," she said, and Nora looked at Miss Misery, for the woman was waving a single hand in the air as she sat upon Mercy.

"Mame?"

"I can't do it right now," Miss Misery said. "Not correctly. I don't have the supplies." She touched her bosom, and Nora knew the tiny snuff bag she kept there held a mixture, but that Miss Misery's true store of herbs and tinctures must have been wherever she lived. Up in the ridge somewhere. In a dark, cool holler. Or a cave maybe?

"It's not far, but you'll have to walk down to the river from here." Miss Misery pointed toward a faint trail. The bridge was behind them, and the rapids far below still clanged like loose coins, reverberating through the valley. "I need wormseed and hawthorn for protection from dishonest forces. Basil for purification. Orange peel and extract for love. I sent up a separation spell before and will need to override that with a binding spell, of course." Miss Misery looked at Nora the whole time she muttered, her eyes glazing over even as Nora watched her tabulate the herbs and powders and potions she would need for the spell to work.

"Separation spell?" As the phrase caught Nora's attention, she only just realized Miss Misery was talking about her and Holly. "Why would you have already sent up a separation spell?"

Miss Misery blinked and her glazed-over eyes—which had rolled up into her eyelids—rolled back as she stared at Nora. Touching her lips, she traced them with her fingertip, and knew the truth was the only way forward. "Because I saw him when he came through."

"Holly?" A car had rolled up to them before slowing to a crawl. As a man and woman looked with awestruck eyes at Nora on the edge of the road, Miss Misery sat perched atop Mercy and waved her hand in the air, pointing.

"I smelled him again. You did, too. You smell him to this moment," and they both lifted their chins as another breeze with whiskey and horse leather saturated the air. "I didn't tell you before, but I came down to the river to keep him away."

"You did what!" Nora's face was red and her heart beat with a raging pulse.

"I thought it best under the circumstances. With Juney having just lost her grandmother, and you losing Holly. I thought the arrival of him again might cast everything into disarray."

"Holy hell, woman—that wasn't your decision to make." Nora had to move to hear it all, and stomped a circle in the dust.

"I know it now. I do. I was wrong, and I'm sorry. But when I saw him dangling through the air, through a circle drawn right above the confluence, I feared he might fall through and drown again and then where would we be?" Miss Misery smiled, and the silvery glow of her lips flashed once, and Nora felt in her body a calmer pulse as the woman paused, shook the reins, before moving off with Mercy as fast as the mule could go.

"That's it?" Nora called to her retreating form, but Miss Misery didn't say anything. Just waved again to the confluence, to where she'd soon return with all her power. And that spell. That binding spell. "That's all you can say after lying to me? Right to my face!"

Silence. It was only the rumbling cart that brought Nora any answer—she had to keep moving. Keep going. So she did, and it was only later, after Nora sat cross-legged on the rocks holding again the candle that she understood. The candle had reignited just like that, once Nora settled into the same spot where Juney had found Holly waterlogged and stunned, river water squelching his boots. *Where the girl had tugged on his hand.* Juney had needed him to help her grandmother. The one too afraid to look at death. The one Holly had helped, and it made Nora think how he'd helped Miss Misery, too. As the candle cast its steady flame across the water, she watched its light rise up to caress the cloud above the confluence. It was the only light that seemed to shimmer on the cloud's glassy skin. And she knew then what Miss Misery had been afraid of. Knew it as sure as sitting there to see the candlelight's warmth and tenderness. The passion Miss Misery had regained—Holly's passion—after all those years of not having it. Seeing him return so soon, falling back into this world, she must have thought she would lose all the love she'd just recovered. *Just like that.* The love she'd been without and so desperately wanted to keep. The same love Nora was determined now more than ever to recapture.

32

THE STABLE WAS COLD AND HOLLY PLUNGED the shovel into mud and horseshit. Lifting it, he saw a deeper layer of soiled hay and heaved it into a wheelbarrow he'd already rolled twice to the waste pile on the other side of the shed row (and downwind from where he worked). He was eighteen. As slim as a beanpole, but strong, and every day getting stronger to do the work no one else wanted to do. But at least he got to be near the horses. At least he got to hear the trainers and jockeys talk. He was beginning to take on the rhythm of their lives—of the life he wanted—and would have shoveled all they asked for the few chances they'd been reluctant enough to give him to ride.

"When they're sick, you're here." Mr. Marvin spoke, Holly at his elbow and following him wherever he went. "When they're too drunk from the night before, you're here. When they can't ride the training session, you're here, and you can ride as long as you don't die on me in the process. You ain't gonna die on me out there, are you, Pride?"

"No, sir. Not unless you want me to."

Mr. Marvin chortled at the answer and ground his teeth looking at the boy. The boy was too tall already, but thin, and the weight was right. He weighed the same as a jockey eight inches shorter, so training rides would be it for him. But Mr. Marvin could tell the boy wanted more. They all did. He wanted to win. To ride across the finish line, flashbulbs bursting in the air. Even a bouquet of roses one day at the Derby. The boy had all the visions and fantasies all the others had. Except this one would never have the chance on account of his height. And maybe that was why Mr. Marvin wasn't as gruff with Holly as he should've been. Why he teased him a bit more than most. Even laughed at his jokes. Grinding the unlit cigar he kept between his teeth no matter the time of day, no matter the occasion.

"Sassafras is ready."

"It's clean?" Mr. Marvin had his clipboard and checked off the name from the list of all the stalls and horses Holly cared for. Each day, petting and brushing their coats when he wasn't shoveling or hauling hay. At night, after working twelve hours, the air in his dreams was crisp, freshly minted, with a rich mineral smell of combed dirt. All the leather polished to a shine, the saddles and stirrups and reins—all of it a smooth assortment of straps and handles. Everything held in his hands, in his dreams. Even the horses' manes waving in the breeze as they rode and he crouched above the horse's ears to feel the rhythm surging through his body. Riding, hovering above the ground. Floating.

Holly noticed a brightening reflection shimmering beneath him. He looked as Callous, Bigs, McCallan, and all the other men leaned over from their seats to see something rising in a shiny flash along the edge of the cloud. Something was encroaching upon their singular space. It was odd—and something Holly felt more than saw. The steady, rising light had its own pull and reminded him of the grayness in the gulley when Clevenger had been astounded to see his shadow again.

"As you were saying?" Bigs slapped his hand on the table, and Holly saw again the shed row and heard Mr. Marvin checking off the horses.

"Paladin?"

"Almost done."

"Your Mother's Keeper?"

"Just about to start."

"It Ain't Misbehavin'?"

"Done and done."

"Then I want you to go to 13." Mr. Marvin looked around when he said it, making sure no one else heard. Shed 13 was where the herbalist worked. The medicine woman. Others called her Misericordia, or Miss Misery, but Holly had only ever handed her the folded-over paper Mr. Marvin gave him and the money. Most times it was a $10 bill. But for some orders, Mr. Marvin would give him $20 and wink, and Holly would wait outside shed 13 for as long as it took the woman to gather the powders and mixtures she handed back without a word. Some of the other stable hands told him she had visions. Sometimes of horses. And could tell the winner before they even posted the odds. Others said she only knew that because she knew which horses were taking her drugs, so of course she knew how they'd do. Nothing mysterious about it.

"How much?"

"I'll tell you how much. And it's for Sarsparilla. For tonight." Mr. Marvin handed Holly a $20 bill and shuffled off.

MONTHS WENT ON LIKE THIS AND HOLLY had found a girl at the soda fountain he liked. A pretty little thing named Nora Grace. *Nora*—the name reminded him of the one he'd met so long ago playing baseball. A girl visiting her cousin all summer. The one he didn't let play. *Was it her?* The same Nora he'd seen on and off throughout his years growing up, but never close enough. Not like this. The one he ordered root beer floats from as often as he could now. The same one he bragged about his riding to. The one who never really said much back, but smiled whenever he came in and already had his root beer float ready by the time he sat at the counter. He bragged to her that he was next in line to be a jockey. That the head trainer for four stables was looking out for him and wouldn't be sending him on chores to Misericordia much longer. "No, mame. I rode Sassafras the other morning, and Sassafras won that night because of it, I guarantee."

"Do you get tips from her, too?"

"Excuse me?"

A man in a suit was seated beside him. Holly hadn't even realized it, but noticed him now that he'd spoken, and especially with Nora shying away from them both. It was odd. He'd never seen her act like that—timid and watchful. It was like she was looking at something from her past and something from her future. Holly was the one from all those years past playing baseball. The one she'd thought about and seen over the years. Sometimes at community dances or at bonfires at the fair ground. But the salesman was the one who loved her, she thought. The one who wanted to be with her, no matter what this trouble was in her belly now. But seeing both men sitting side by side set such a queer look on her face, Holly had a notion to reach over and touch her, even as the man tapped his shoulder and leaned in to say something. Which usually meant there might be some money involved.

"I hear she knows who's going to win before they even run. That she sings their names out. Like a ritual or something. Is that true?"

"She does have a way; I can attest."

"Well, I'll tell you what, I have a list here of some herbs I need. Someone else put it together for me, but I need someone like her, what'd you say—Misericordia— someone who knows herbs and tinctures, and how to put them together. And I don't need anyone asking any questions about it neither."

Nora was watching; Holly could see her eyes—they were pinched and concentrated. The man leaning over was whispering in his ear, but Holly's eyes were focused on her. She was sad, and rubbed her belly once when the man started talking, before looking away.

"That might cost you some, sir," Holly said.

"Whatever it costs, no problem. I represent investors, son. Investors who I've spoken to recently about horses. I believe they might be interested in owning one."

"*Investors?*" Holly couldn't see Nora anymore. As soon as he heard that word, he closed his eyes and let the idea roll through his body, until all he saw was the horse's mane. The ears he leaned over. His hands on the reins. His body a slick blade cutting the air.

"And we could sure use a jockey once we buy." The man patted Holly's shoulder, and the vision broke. Handing him a list of ingredients, the man included a $50 bill.

IT WAS LIKE ANY OTHER NIGHT WHEN HOLLY waited outside shed 13 on his errand for that businessman. Holly never did ask his name. Funny. It didn't matter though, he thought. *He had investors! And they needed a jockey!* Holly had walked on two feet of air that whole week, figuring he'd have to let Mr. Marvin know soon that he was moving on. Though he did appreciate all of Mr. Marvin's help and advice. Maybe he could even put in a word for Mr. Marvin with the new investors, have him be the trainer or something. The night was just settling in, and Holly could feel the energy of the crowd starting to gather. The grandstands were filling up for the first race, and the sound of it all buzzed through the air and set his skin alight. Goosebumps raised up on his arms, and he was excited for the life he saw unspooling before him when the door creaked open, and he expected the same hand to thrust out a brown paper bag with his order. But only darkness appeared.

"Mame?" he said and stepped closer, as the tall, thin woman came into focus. Her hair was a dark wave brushed back, her eyes smeared with charcoal or burnt cork. A smell not unlike sour milk wafted off her as she loomed just a few inches from him.

"Tansy, safflower, and wild celery all mixed with bitter water. It is a particular mixture. One I don't often give out."

"It's for a friend, mame." Holly held his hand out, and grabbing it, she turned it over to see the palm, and Holly shivered to feel the icy sensation race through him. She might have been made of snow crystals, and he swore he saw his breath hover between them in the warm night air. Tracing a line on his palm, she followed it from his wrist to his middle finger where it stopped.

"You have an unusual fate. And somehow, I always knew I'd be part of it. I just didn't know how large a part until tonight." Only then had she tilted her head up to stare into his eyes. A look that held him speechless. That made him see himself from far off, when he was older. He was dripping wet and shivering, and he could see shadows and an eerie collection of luminous lines comprising everything. He was in the woods with her. On a hillside. And she was leaning in for a kiss.

"Oh, shit shit," Holly said and was startled from his vision. Shuddering atop Callous, the mule jumped and came back down, thundering amongst the churning airy currents. All the images stretched around them collapsed into glossy black shadows of hills and stars and trees. Holly saw again the light shimmering beneath the cloud. It stretched up to cover the whole side of their space now. "Of course," he said, "it was her—but younger. Why didn't I know that? Why didn't I see? She wasn't only the woman I gave my passion to. She was the one who gave Nora the potion to take a baby off, the baby she must have had with that businessman."

33

NORA SWAYED SITTING ALONE AND WATCHED the candlelight and heard the sounds she knew she'd hear as soon as it lit itself again. Voices in the woods echoed far off, but came closer. Oars churned out on the Shenandoah. She heard the same thudding sound of wooden hulls against rocks and saw the faint outline of boats approaching—the same ones who'd been down here with her before. They were all being gathered again by the candlelight. And she wasn't sure if that was what Miss Misery wanted, not with what they planned to do, and wondered what she would say to make them leave. At least, the ones on foot. She did need a boat, and smiled at the man who rowed to a halt at the rock she held the candle on.

"I just heard a."

"I know." Nora held the candle higher so the man could scramble ashore. He looked at her once as if to say something, but then found a soft patch of sand and sat down cross-legged, let out one long sigh, and just watched the candle.

"Well, I didn't think it would ever."

"I just knew it was what I thought it was, but."

"How could it be so true, but also be so."

Three shapeless figures on the edge of the woods stepped closer as their voices died down. It was three women Nora recognized from the other day. Three women who'd sat and bowed their heads and clasped their hands in prayer until the police showed up and chased everyone away.

"Welcome," Nora said, and everyone looked at her because she'd never spoken before, and the few others still approaching along the banks nodded their heads as if they needed, or rather—expected—more this time. "You may not know me, and that's fine. I'm still not sure what the candlelight is able to do, but it seems to speak to each of us in a way that each of us needs."

A general hum of agreement met her comments. A few more folks had gathered in the dark by the water. All told, maybe two dozen folks had heard the candlelight enough inside them to come out into the middle of the night, scampering through tree roots and underbrush and rolling rapids to be here.

"I wanted to thank you for believing enough to come out even without any warning. The candle just lit itself up without me even knowing."

Nora heard an audible gasp when she said this, and then a hushed and reverent calm. A stillness took over the clearing, and Nora wasn't sure if it was a hush enlivened by the thoughts and energies of those gathered about, or if the candlelight had attained some higher frequency. There was a shimmering in the air above them. It flashed and roiled like a campfire, weaving its strands on the cloud suspended high above the confluence, fifty yards out in the river.

"I lost my husband out there," she said. "Three days ago, he drowned. But somehow, he gave me this candle the same night—after he died." Holding the candle higher, Nora stood and watched the cloud gather in more light and reflect it back like a beacon. "I don't hear anything when I look at the flame. I don't see anything inside it. I don't taste anything I've lost. I don't feel anything except my Holly. I feel how close he still is, and I know that maybe he can see the candle whenever it's lit. That it connects us across whatever divide there is."

"I hear my daughter laughing, before she fell ill."

"I smell my parents. Their close, familiar woodstove smell."

"I'm held by it. I can't describe it any other way."

"It sings to me, but I've already told you that."

Nora heard the girl's voice and looked at the folks gathered before her and the few who'd spoken, but she couldn't see her. Then she remembered the way they'd went to the cave with Ruddy, and when she turned, Juney was walking toward her wearing the same blue overalls. With the same tangle of impossible hair overflowing and bouncing with each step.

"Juney," Nora said, and held her for a long moment. As Nora rocked the girl in her arms, she wanted right then to push the girl with all her strength inside her, so that no one else could take her. Then she couldn't get hurt by death or life or disappointment. She'd forever be latched to her body no matter what the police tried to do or say. "You ran away?"

"Of course, I did. They were ignorant there. Never did listen to what I said. I told them about your situation. Told them a dead man visited me, too. Told them he was your husband. That he gave his eyes to my grandmother so she could see. Gave his heart away, too, apparently. Well, you can imagine how that went."

Nora couldn't help but smile as the girl went on, rambling out her frustrations.

"They tried to give me a pill before they shut me up in my room. But I faked it. I didn't swallow it when they thought I did. I suppose they were knocking me out. Thought it was the trauma of the whole ordeal that made me speak so. Inventing visions. As if. I left as soon as they turned off the lights and shut the door."

"I knew exactly where you meant in your note." Nora held the paper in her other hand and then put it back in her apron pocket. "We buried her just like you wanted. Put her in the dress and hat you'd laid out. Miss Misery even spoke with her, Ester. She was the one who told us you were in the orphanage. Even said she was happy to be back with your grandfather."

"With Pap Pap Pete?" Juney wiped the tears from her face and looked at the crowd and wondered how long it would be before the police showed.

"I know," Nora sensed the girl's unease, and leaned closer so only Juney could hear. "Miss Misery's coming back with a spell. We're going to try and bring that cloud down," and Nora pointed above the confluence.

Juney shivered seeing the object she hadn't been able to notice until it was pointed out to her. "How long has that been there?"

"You mean, you hadn't seen it?" Nora looked at everyone seated before her. What could they see? What did they know? "Sometimes I don't know if this is real. Any of it." Nora was speaking louder—and either by design or impulse—her words and tone were darker. And on a few moments as she scoured the eyes of those gathered before her, she saw women and men flinch to look upon her. They were scared, and in this way, she thought she might drive them away for the privacy they needed, and so dug deeper into that sinister well. "I looked and there was a dead man at my back. He was hovering there, and his eyes were gone, and a hole in his chest sucked in and out as the breeze blew through him. And his lips. I couldn't touch his lips, but there was such a lonesomeness upon them. As if all the silvery love had been pulled from deep inside. These last hours I've buried a woman, too. Made her up pretty but placed her six feet under so her soul could move on. And even then, the woman I was with—whom some of you might know—Miss Misery," and another audible gasp rose over all those gathered. "Miss Misery spoke to the dead woman as easy as I'm speaking now. I've asked her to come here, too."

"The dead woman?"

"Miss Misery?"

"The witch?"

"Yes," Nora said, and some of the women stood and started to gather their things to know that Miss Misery would soon be amongst their number. "I asked her to come and be with us. To delight in these moments of life that seem so closely twined to these moments of death. So she can see inside each of you. She can see what there is ahead of you and what there is behind."

A branch snapped as Nora finished, and a dozen heads startled to look behind. A bright silver flame pulsed as it moved down through the trees, and the folks cried out now that it was the police come back again to get them for good. But it wasn't the police they saw. The silver flame pulsed brighter, pulsing from a torch that wavered high above and lit up her hair and long, curvy shape. Her black dress glinting here and there with silver luminescent threads.

"It's her—Miss Misery! It's the witch!"

34

HOLLY COULDN'T SPEAK OR MOVE AS THE JURY discussed the last realization he'd made about the herbs he'd acquired for Nora. The herbs he'd gotten for the woman who'd one day become his wife. Herbs that when taken in the prescribed way would take off the unborn child she carried from that businessman. A man who couldn't be bothered to have another dependent with some side piece he kept in Charles Town. Just like all the others he'd probably strung along throughout his sales territory. In Roanoke, Chantilly, Winchester, and Richmond. Simple. They were all simple and young and had wanted more than what their lives had given them. To get out into the world, and this wasn't the first time he'd made this purchase. But now, Holly knew inside it was Nora's child. The one he hadn't been able to give her in life. But now in death—to know it was the same child he'd taken from her—made the bulge in his chest throb as the new heart beat faster, and the sweat lined his brow when he thought of Nora losing what she'd always wanted so early in life. And he understood now the urgency that had simmered beneath the surface of their marriage. An urgency he was never able to satisfy.

You didn't know. The voice came to Holly, and he couldn't be bothered to answer, acknowledging the significance of what Misericordia had told him. That it was a particular mixture. One she didn't often give out. *How could you know? He used you. He heard you bragging that you knew the woman. That you had dealings with her before. And he played on your desire to ride.*

"It was only when she read my palm that she agreed." Holly felt Callous trotting beneath him. Felt the rhythm of the mule rising and falling and patted his neck. It was Callous speaking to him. Callous easing his fear. Callous understanding the absurdity of his impossible position—of not knowing what the man wanted the herbs for. "Of not caring," Holly countered. "I didn't care enough to understand. I only thought of riding that horse. Of racing and becoming a jockey because of his investors. Shit. Nora."

Bigs had watched all of this and was listening. McCallan too. The other men were still arguing and curious about the information Holly had recovered that wasn't in the file. *So much wasn't in the file.* "Any word yet?" Bigs looked at McCallan, and standing on his chair, McCallan looked over the heads of the other men at some indistinct destination and shook his head.

"Nothing."

"Did we even ask Holly to call him?"

"Christ. We didn't."

Holly understood immediately. He remembered giving his wedding ring to Edison all that time ago. As payment for something. *Passage? Understanding?* He wasn't sure. But he was certain that Edison told him to call for anything he needed. And right now, he needed the truth.

"Edison!" Silence. Holly looked at Bigs, at McCallan, at all the other men who'd stopped their bickering to concentrate on Holly's voice. A certain quality in it had disrupted every other sound. Had sculpted some piercing power, so that Holly could almost see his voice align into a single cord that wound its way through whatever substance contained them, at whatever level they'd been suspended. "Edison! I need you!"

A sound much like a train thundering along its tracks bellowed out and screeched. Then, with an overly dramatic burst of wind Edison appeared standing beside the table—his hat in his hand. "You called?"

"We've been looking for you." Crossing his arms, Bigs glared as Edison fumbled with his hat before bowing and nodding. As he did, Holly could make out a large rectangular flap in the middle of his bald head. It was loose and slapped against his skull until he had to smooth the flap down with his hand. The man was full of replacement parts as well.

"I had trouble finding my way back," Edison countered. "It's not easy making it through the levels to the file cabinets and then back again. I can assure you."

"Oh, boo hoo," Bigs snarled.

"It's not easy either, seeing all this." Looking around, Edison saw the dark mountains, the stars, the lights of Harpers Ferry and sighed.

"It's been a while for us, too." Bigs looked with McCallan and all the others at the scenery, and Holly could feel that all along, they weren't angry at him for bringing them here. They were wistful. They all wanted to be down there in the water or on the banks, feeling the wind, seeing the colors of the leaves. Tasting raindrops and whiskey—*real whiskey*—not whatever it was they drank in their fake burlesque, in some made-up room on some low-grade level in whatever labyrinth contained them. They all looked at Holly as if following his thoughts. They were envious of him. Because maybe he had a chance to go back and complete whatever it was he had to do to hear the calling again—*his calling*—and maybe it would end up with him rising higher than where they'd been stranded for so long. "Mr. Hollis Pride has graced us with the details of his three incidents."

"Has he now?"

"Stalling. He's stalling." Holly pointed at Edison and the man smiled an impish grin, and Callous lunged at him, snapping his brown cracked teeth.

"*Jesus!*" Edison ducked beneath Callous and dropped his hat, before standing closer to the table. He was close enough that Bigs reached across and grabbed his wrist.

"Where is it?" Bigs held Edison's hand and turned it over. Nothing. Bigs grabbed Edison's left hand and pulled, and the whole hand came off, and a few jurors chuckled to see it: Edison with a stump where his hand should have been. "Christ, it's not here either." Bigs was about to toss Edison's hand back when McCallan stopped him.

"You know what we're looking for," McCallan snapped.

"Of course. The ring," Edison spoke, and Holly couldn't help but look at his stump, and he wondered how many other parts the man had scrounged up over the eons. And why was the ring so important?

"The truth. That's what the ring symbolizes," Bigs said, anticipating Holly's confusion. "It symbolizes true love. That which binds Holly and Nora—from the past—into the future. I think you made a mistake accepting it." Bigs was stepping around the table toward Edison. As he moved, he drained the last drops of his glass and stood beside Callous. "There was certainly something else you could have taken."

"*There wasn't anything else of value*," Edison hissed.

"Then why take anything at all?" Bigs said.

"Why not just do your job?" McCallan added.

"Then how would I get anything to barter with? How else can we ascend without our bodies intact? You all do it," and Edison scowled at the hypocrisy, but still wasn't sure what Bigs had in mind. Holly could feel each eye upon him. Bigs was motioning toward Holly's undershirt (for that was all Holly still had to wear—his undershirt and boxer shorts and blue and black argyle socks; he'd discarded his suit of river water in opening the portal).

"Just wring it out a bit. Here." Bigs held up his whiskey glass, and Holly touched his shirt and realized he was still sopping wet. Wringing out the bottom half of his shirt, it filled up half the glass with river water. Bigs then tipped the glass so that it was ready to pour onto Edison's detached left hand, which Bigs held up, showing everyone. "Where's the ring? Where's the missing information in his file? For the three incidents."

Edison smirked and was silent. Shrugging his shoulders, Bigs poured a thin stream of river water onto Edison's left hand, onto the ring finger.

At once, Edison writhed with pain and grasped his stump. The ring finger smoldered as a red band of flesh at the base of the finger—where the ring had resided—blistered and puckered, so that the skin looked ready to burst. "*Jesus!* I don't know! I honestly don't!"

"You do realize his shirt and underwear will always be wet? He's drowned until he hears the calling. That won't change," McCallan said. "We could do this forever."

Holly patted his shirt, and it was sopping wet, just as it had been before he wrung out the bottom half.

Bigs continued. "Where's the ring? We want to hear it speak."

"I said, I don't know!"

Bigs poured again, and again the fleshy band blistered under the liquid, until a yellowy stream ran from the finger over the hand and wrist. "Jesus, Bigs, now I'll have to get another hand!" Edison was on his knees, his left arm held against his stomach, as he bowed beneath Callous. "Of course, I changed it. Erased the file. The ring—*the true ring*—could have gotten me a spot in the next level. You know that. You *all* know that. I was waiting to trade it at the next big swap." Edison glared at Bigs, before eying each member of the jury.

"You bastard! My death is at stake." Holly leaned toward Edison as Callous snorted; the mule was ready to stomp on Edison if Holly only nodded.

"Are you kidding?" Edison said, and looked at Holly. "You're lucky I got it. Don't you think he wanted it for himself? What do you suppose he told Clevenger to hack off first?"

"Lies!" Bigs stood over Edison, and McCallan had to hold him back.

"But it doesn't matter anymore. None of us can use it. It's gone now."

"You fool!" Bigs cried as the jury clamored for answers.

"On my way back, I heard something in the river far below, while you idiots were arguing. Something light and warm rose up to me and sung with the softest truth. It told me that I'd lose it forever if I kept it, that you'd take it from me, and that none of you cared for anything I've ever done. My tears opened up the smallest portal beneath me. So I threw it down where you could never get it. I threw it in the river."

35

THE ROWBOAT WOBBLED AND NORA leaned on the oars as Juney passed Miss Misery the ingredients. In the middle of her muttering incantation, her eyes had glazed over, and her arms were raised to the swirling darkness. But in the next instant, she'd call for dried frog legs, or crushed anise seeds, or fresh henbane, and Juney would reach into the knapsack Miss Misery had brought, find the labeled ingredient (if it was labeled), and hand it to the woman. Juney then watched awestruck as the woman knelt in the bow and stirred everything in a black volcanic pot she'd lugged down with her, before continuing in whatever language she spoke. The whole time, her incantation was agitating the wind and rapids into parting before them on the haphazard way Nora had to paddle to bring them closer to the confluence. The night had passed in a blink. After Miss Misery had arrived, scattering the people from the candlelight, Nora pointed at a man who'd rowed his boat to the gathering, and that was enough. Miss Misery touched his arm, and he smiled at her as listless as a puppy. The woman was just dripping with passion. Silver puddles of it pooled in her eyes and mouth, and Nora wondered if they'd even need the dawn's light to guide them. They could just use Miss Misery's pulsing love.

"Just look at her," Nora said to Juney, as they put everything in the boat and the man stood there entranced.

"You can go now." Miss Misery waved, and he stumbled off the way the others had gone when they'd been frightened by Miss Misery's approach.

"It's about the only thing I can look at," Juney said, and stared with Nora who couldn't stop pointing. The woman was already in the bow waving her arms, muttering, building a labyrinth of sounds and spells, as something in her voice echoed across the water.

"The passion. It's just dripping from her. And it wasn't like this on the road." Nora nodded to consider it, how the fountain of Holly's passion must have been bubbling up with them being so close to wherever he was.

"She's all silver." Juney sat in the middle of the boat, and was already being ordered to produce orange rinds and sassafras root.

"*The bird's nest*," Nora whispered, and pushed off with an oar, before settling in the stern. She touched her belly before paddling. The bird's nest must have still been in there, letting her see and feel things she had no right to see and feel. Like that cloud—or bubble—the shimmering side of which the candlelight lit up. She had set the candle on the seat beside her, and was stunned to see it not move an inch, even as they were battered by rocks while she first rowed up the Shenandoah, pulling against the current, closer to the point where Harpers Ferry had been carved out by the confluence of the Shenandoah and Potomac. Then she would drift down the forty yards to the rapids where she knew Holly had drowned. Where that cloud hovered high above, shining from the candlelight on the western side and the dawn's rising light on the eastern side.

"Wormseed," Miss Misery called, and Juney had no idea what wormseed was and reached into the knapsack, trusting she'd find whatever Miss Misery needed.

"Here." Juney handed over a slick black pouch, and Miss Misery weighed it in her hand, nodded her head, and smiled at Juney.

"Now artemisia. You might know it by mugworts; I need the oil. There should be a bottle." Miss Misery smiled again and knelt above the cauldron as the boat careened off a rock, and Nora yelled "*Shit, shit!*" But all of it was inconsequential compared to the feeling welling up inside Miss Misery, with her passion. Francis had been there, at her home. Waiting, of course. Of all the outlandish events of the past few days, this had been the one that had stopped Miss Misery in her tracks. Her Francis sitting in his Ford sedan, the front door open, the car still on, the brand-new radio he'd installed playing "Did You Ever See a Dream Walking?" and Bing Crosby's voice booming across the front porch. It was beautiful. She'd felt like he'd been waiting all his life for her. That the chance occurrence of Francis lending his boat to Hollis hadn't been just that—a coincidence—but an event ordained by the machination of the stars. And that she'd been waiting all this time since her Eddie died at that damn soda fountain for something as pure, as true. *The fool*, trying to rob a few extra dollars for their elopement. To get her out from working the shed row at the track. But now another man had understood that surprising her like this—with something romantic playing—on a soft, unobtrusive night was what went straight to her heart. It cut through all the spells and incantations and tinctures that had layered over her feelings with the sad discoveries she had to make about other people's lives. "But what's my life?" she said, after they listened to the song play all the way through. She was in the passenger seat. Her hand in his. He hadn't said anything. Just watched her. "Why do I get to see into other people's lives, into what they want and need, but not my own?"

"Just lucky, I guess?" Smiling, Francis kissed her. He leaned across just like that. Another song had started, and Miss Misery felt his lips on hers and forgot all about the cloud hovering above the confluence, about Juney and Nora and the task at hand. There was only warmth in her like there hadn't been in years. Love pulsed inside her, like the silvery strands of her passion. And when Francis leaned away—awestruck by the kiss—she saw several strands dangling from his lips. That was what snapped her back into action. She didn't want to think about Francis being influenced by Hollis Pride's passion anymore. She didn't want him influenced by anything other than her own love, which she hadn't given away like this to anyone since Eddie. *Determination*—that was what got her out of that passenger seat. It also had her holding up a hand to Francis, hushing him from saying anything else.

"Later. I promise." Gathering the ingredients happened in a blur. Francis sulked a bit in his car through another two songs, turning up the volume so that the whole hillside must have heard the refrain of "Just an Echo in the Valley," another Bing Crosby tune. But all of that had to wait. She barked to Juney another ingredient, and all she could hear was the rough sound of Francis's car turning in the grass, before the rocks spit out from his back tires as he sped off.

"Hold on!" Nora held an oar up and was bracing for impact, before Juney jumped closer to help. They pushed with the oar against the oncoming rock. The boat sloughed off through the rushing water, and Nora patted Juney's arm and could see the cloud almost above them. There was no time to consider where to bring the boat, and for a moment, she understood why Holly had drowned here, why he'd had so much trouble maneuvering. She wasn't sure they would make it, and that was with whatever help Miss Misery's incantations were doing to part the waters. Because the river seemed to be deciding that now, too—if they would make it—even as Miss Misery called out for basil and owl feather and bat wing and silver.

"*Silver?*" Juney handed the other ingredients over and looked again in the knapsack and nothing came to meet her fingers.

The volcanic sides of the cauldron spit and flared with a ghostly flame, and lit Miss Misery from below with a green light that lent an air of credence to what the women on shore had called her: *the witch.* Nora shivered seeing it, but was also calmed by the concoction's smell. For just then, a breeze wafted from the bow and brought the scent of root beer to her nose—*root beer?*—after all those ingredients had merged and swirled together. Nora shook her head and brought the boat to the best place she could find, wedged in-between two large boulders, atop a mass of jagged rocks. The cloud was right above them. The underside was glassy and swirled with the two lights meeting in it. The candlelight had merged with the dawn, and the result brought out a golden glow on the whole underside. It looked like what Nora thought a pregnant belly would look like, right before birth. Golden and bulging and fortified with veins of an underlying construction.

"*Silver!*" Miss Misery cried again, and Juney shook her head, and Nora heard nothing but an airy swoosh. Looking up, she saw how it glinted at her, and she wasn't sure how time had slowed in that instant, but the moment had seemed to slow for Juney, too. And with a nod from Nora, Juney had the composure and steadiness and calm to reach up, spreading out her palm—and Holly's wedding ring landed there as softly as could be. At once, Juney saw the dead man. Nora could see him, too, felt the smooth, cool metal against the girl's flesh. Tears lined Nora's cheek, for she knew she wouldn't have been able to hand the ring over if she'd touched it. But she nodded, and Juney handed it to Miss Misery, who muttered one final charm, before tossing it in.

36

THE AIRY RAPIDS THAT CALLOUS HAD GALLOPED in this whole time began to sputter and pop. Then Holly felt a great shudder along the entire length of the cloud. As Bigs and McCallan and the other jurors looked down, Holly had never seen fear in their eyes like this. Even Edison's pained smirk dissolved as the first shivering earthquake shook the airy egg beneath them.

"It's the ring!" Bigs looked at Holly and stumbled from behind the table. "The ring did this!" Holly looked and the long table had been split in two. Its long central spine shivered and twisted, before the two halves calved off like a glacier in meltwater.

"The cloud!" McCallan pointed, and the imperceptible edge—the one they'd all seen and known, but which was nearly invisible with the mountains and stars showing through—was dripping from the top down. The bubble had a long, sagging hole in it. Another thunderous charge had burst below them, and all the water from the airy rapids Callous had been galloping in started draining in a raging waterfall to the confluence.

I can see her. Callous snorted, and Holly understood and looked through the hole spreading beneath them.

"Nora. And Misericordia. And the girl—the one I gave my eyes to!" Holly saw them in a boat wedged into the same rocks that had sucked him under. And for a moment, he remembered the pressure. His hands against the gritty soil; a substance not unlike milk drifting from them. Then all he could feel was his stuck left foot. It was pressed against Callous. Even as he felt the instinct to jump, Callous had lumbered up on his back legs, and it made Holly press closer to the mule's neck, grabbing tighter.

I wouldn't advise jumping just yet. The words Callous spoke vibrated through Holly's chest as he watched a silver stream bursting up from a black cauldron.

155

Misericordia stood in the boat and had her arms and head raised. Holly could see her eyes like when she'd handed him the herbs in the shed row. He looked at Nora when he remembered and watched her hunch forward, her hands on her stomach.

"Nora!" he screamed, but the silver stream from the cauldron blasted with such force, a riot of water and steam started melting the sides of the cloud, she could have never heard him.

"This is all your fault!" Bigs stood above Edison and grabbed his throat. "If you hadn't thrown down that ring! If you hadn't accepted it in the first place!" All the jurors could see Miss Misery—and as if in unison—they listened to her muttering voice and were afraid. It was a language they all knew but could never speak. Most were on their knees watching her, even as beneath them the thin, cloudy membrane dripped and sagged. Until the first part of the airy rapids Callous lumbered in fell, evaporating into nothing as soon as it breached the living realm.

Poof! Another airy shape and another disappeared, and most of the jurors looked at each other with a helpless sadness, as cloudy parts plummeted for only a moment before dissolving into nothing.

"Christ, after all these years of waiting and trading."

"Of trading and waiting."

"And listening to Bigs."

"And McCallan."

"Telling us this was the way it was."

"How it *always* was."

"To trust the process of waiting and trading."

"Of trading and waiting."

"All these lifetimes wasted."

"Just to be turned into that."

"Into what?"

"When we're so close to being balanced."

"Rising another level."

Another chunk of airy rapids slipped through, vanishing in a cloudy mist. But this time, a small whispering siren sounded, and none of them knew what it meant, but they kept looking. Kept kneeling. Kept hoping it wasn't for them, this final airy conclusion.

"All I needed was a liver."

"I needed just a pinky toe."

"Jesus, just a pinky toe."

"Can you imagine—a stupid pinky toe."

"All I needed was an appendix. You don't even *need* an appendix. So why should I have to worry about finding another appendix to go higher?"

"Yeah, but a pinky toe. Come on. It's not even an organ."

There was a moment that Holly saw their eyes. There were ten of them from the jury. They teetered in the void as the last airy chunk beneath Callous tumbled through. Then, en masse—all ten of them—slipped into the living, breathing world and seemed astonished to feel the early sunlight rising across the valley. To smell the river smells and warm earthen smells of someone cooking somewhere. Maybe fresh-caught catfish for breakfast. With biscuits and pancakes and maple syrup, too. With salt and butter and toast. Taste touched their tongues again. The taste of breathing. Of air. Of light. Of sky. Of river. Of food. Of *real* food. Of the hours and minutes passing in an orderly flow. Of time not measured out in eons, but in moments you moved through. Moments that ended and meant something by ending. They were ending now and knew it, even if they thought no one could ever really end. Had been told that or believed it. Told there was a balance in all of the odd parts and levels of the airy Above, as well as in the arid Below. That whomever designed it all had started out with a scaffolding built over the eventual design, but had liked the scaffolding so much the design *became* the scaffolding, with its levels and ladders and endless risings and fallings to other indecipherable levels. And there always needed to be a balance of bodies here and there and there. There was something oddly geometric to it, they never cared to follow to its conclusion. To its ending. To what it meant now to watch the silver stream from that black cauldron spray them with its pronouncement—and in a large, groaning pulse—they all blinked out once and then back on, as if the world were one vast light switch, before blinking off into oblivion.

Hold on! Callous snorted, and Edison, Bigs, and McCallan each grabbed ahold of a hoof, and by either touching Callous, or in being connected to Holly and the task he still had to complete, all five of them lurched out into the living realm—into the clear air above the valley—and proceeded to fall headlong toward Nora and Juney, toward Miss Misery and the rowboat waiting below them at the confluence.

PART IV:
IN THE TREE, ALWAYS

37

NORA'S STOMACH HURT AND HAD HER BENT over wondering what force Miss Misery had unleashed to see the cauldron spew up like that. The gurgling stream must have shot up a full ten seconds before the cloud gurgled and dripped and sludged into a broken, splintered mess. It then rained down on them in watery shards and chunks before she saw the legs of a mule. Like sliding from a crack at the bottom of an egg. There were three men attached to the mule's hindquarters. They seemed dumbstruck by the chain of events that had them hovering fifty feet above the rapids, suspended for the longest moment, until Holly appeared atop the mule. Then, all at once, the great tangled shape fell through—and she could feel it as they fell—that Holly's eyes and heart had been returned to him. His heart beat the same rhythm as hers, and her stomach unclenched to hear it. She felt it even as they splashed down beside the rapids, with most of them landing in a pool of water that was deep enough they were lucky they weren't all smashed to bits on the rocks. One of them didn't fare as well as the rest.

"Edison?" A small man with red hair and bushy sideburns had reached up to touch Edison's left hand, or where the man's left hand should've been. But the man had nothing left to say. He'd landed with his back on a wide rock where a jagged center stone jutted up. There wasn't any blood, but a bluebird appeared from somewhere and hovered above him, twittering a sad, curious song, and the unnatural slant in his torso told them all they needed to know.

Nora, Miss Misery, and Juney watched with the rest of them as Edison dissolved, puffed up into a pile of ash, and was blown asunder in the next breeze. Holly didn't seem too concerned about it. He was still seated atop Callous, and was too dazed from falling into a pool of water atop a mule to wonder at seeing a man blown to ash beside him. Not with Nora standing right there in a boat, her heart thrumming in rhythm to his. "Nora? I can see you!" Smiling, Holly pointed at his eyes as Nora's body forced her to go to him, to step from the stern to the bow, but Juney had to hold her steady.

"You're here?" Nora muttered, blinking her eyes. "It's impossible," as she stretched with all her might to reach him. But the rush of water that arrived once the mule and men had fallen through had unmoored their boat. Nora stretched and stretched for Holly—who was just ten feet away—but in a moment he was twenty, then fifty, as the boat twisted backward through the rapids.

"The oars!" Miss Misery had been shaken to her knees by the thudding progress of the backward boat. The cauldron sizzled beside her as the last remains of the spell spit out a few silvery sparks. Nora couldn't move. Was too connected to Holly—to his new blue eyes—to do anything. So Juney had to be the one to pull the oars up and turn the boat around. Juney had to be the one to keep them from shattering to pieces.

"Follow them!" Holly screamed, and Callous was already treading out from the deep pool, Bigs and McCallan trailing from his tail. They were still afraid they might dissolve like Edison if they weren't touching Callous, if they weren't somehow connected to Holly's task. It was flowing through them now, Holly's pulsing heartbeat. They felt it vibrating through the river as Callous floated out and scrambled now and then in the shallows as they chased the rowboat. Holly was meant to be here for something. For Nora, most likely, and as Bigs and McCallan considered it all and looked at Holly, they were astonished to feel the cold, rushing water.

"It's perfect!" Bigs said, and dragged a hand through the brisk current.

"I never thought I'd be back." McCallan was crying, but Holly couldn't tell because the man was too busy dunking his head beneath the surface. As he looked beneath the water, minnows and trout scattered from the scrambling shape of them.

"I never thought I'd miss it this much." Bigs was teary too. "I believe we owe you an apology," and they both stared at Holly. "Thank you for whatever it is you have to do. Thank you."

Holly couldn't take his eyes from Nora. The girl had been able to turn the boat around, and Holly nudged Callous to follow. They were headed to the Maryland side, where the towpath and C&O Canal could be seen at intervals through the trees. The current was slower there, but Holly knew from just the other day the river was up and ran with more force and danger in the days before he decided to go fishing. *Christ.* Fishing. For what? Just so he could be away from Nora. So he wouldn't have to walk into that quiet house and think about her asking him again about adopting a child. When all he heard in her voice was a lonesomeness. A sorrow at not being a mother. And his failure at not providing for her. *The candle.* When Holly thought of his failure, he realized the candle he'd given to Nora was burning throughout all this. He looked and Nora was in the boat watching him, the candle beside her, its steady beacon calling to him with a voice he couldn't understand. He knew there were words in the light. They were comforting at times, and in the next moment, challenging. They were also focused on him and what he had to do. But the language of it. The out-of-focus language. It was here and not here. Like he was here and not here. Like *they* were here and not here. He looked at Bigs and McCallan and Callous and wondered how much time they had before they all dissolved, too?

"There you are!"

Holly heard the voice far off, a voice echoing over the water. He could tell it wasn't Nora or the girl or Misericordia. *Jesus,* that woman. He didn't even want to look at her. Whatever spell she'd cast—a spell powerful enough to overcome a cloud of otherworldly import—was enough for him. There was no telling what else she might want, and tracing his lips, he remembered what she'd already taken.

"Look—we all have shadows here!"

Shadows? Holly was certain he hadn't told anyone about the dry riverbed and grayness he'd been forced to trudge through. Only the mule and maybe Bigs and McCallan knew about that. The mule whose legs were floating again as they found a deeper section on the Maryland side. Beyond them, the rowboat was coming to shore so easily. The girl was good at it, Holly saw. She rowed and steered all at once, before finding a tree root stretched into the shallows. The root created a kind of shelf in the mud, a landing spot where the rowboat could rest and where they all could scramble up the riverbank. *But the voice?* It was familiar.

"Ahoy!" The voice boomed again and was unmistakable to Bigs and McCallan, who dared to look from where they floated attached to Callous.

"How in Christ?"

"I'm at a loss for words." Bigs just pointed then, and Holly followed his arm to the riverbanks where a man stood in dripping rags. A dead man, most certainly. He had that sort of blue edge that all the dead had here, rounded in a blurry focus.

"How's it possible?" Holly spoke, and Callous shuddered beneath him to see the man they both thought had drowned when they first fell through. Clevenger waved to them from land.

38

FROM THE SHALLOWS WHERE CALLOUS AND HOLLY, Bigs and McCallan stood, Clevenger smiled as he stepped closer to the river. It was interesting to feel the cold shiver through their bodies. All the drops of river water Holly had been so used to since dying, were that much more reinforced by floating for almost half an hour. His teeth chattered, and his arms and legs shook, and as he stared at his wife, he listened to the indecipherable voice in the candle. Nora, the girl, and Miss Misery (for he'd heard Nora call her that after they'd left the boat) seemed unable to come any closer. They couldn't move past Clevenger, even though Holly got the sense that Nora's body wasn't in any hurry to approach him anymore. Something wouldn't let them reach out to each other, to combine the depth of their thoughts and feelings. Something held them apart.

"Don't say my name. Don't say any of our names." Clevenger smiled and patted Callous, smoothing his hand along the mule's neck. The men and mule had climbed as one from the river to the banks, then through the twenty yards of brush and thicket to the towpath beside the canal. Bigs and McCallan the whole time had kept a hand touching Callous. Even on the towpath as they walked and Clevenger laughed at the ridiculousness of their conviction, they refused to let go. "Come now. It's not the mule that's kept you here. And he certainly couldn't keep you from Edison's fate either—being blown to ash."

"How do you know?" Bigs had regained a certain measure of authority in seeing Clevenger—his clear subordinate from that other realm—walking and talking in the living realm.

"Well, I saw it all, didn't I?" Clevenger swept his arm toward the confluence a half mile north of where they walked. The train tracks were on the other side of the canal. Nora, Miss Misery, and Juncy had kept pace with the slow progress of the mule, staying ten yards in front of them the whole time. Nora had decided to walk backward so she could watch Holly, but still felt the separation they had to keep. Something like an invisible barrier held them apart. "It might have been easier if you'd just announced it to the whole world with the noise of that thing, crashing down in a rain of watery shards."

Bigs made a sideways glance at Miss Misery, and McCallan caught his drift and did the same, so that Clevenger understood what they meant without a word.

"Of course, I knew it was her. What with that cauldron and the spell she cast." Clevenger pointed at Miss Misery, and she glared at the man, and even though he was dead, he flinched to see the anger she fixed upon him.

"Subtlety was never your strong point." Bigs slapped Clevenger's arm, and Clevenger's ragged shirt squelched beneath the man's hand.

"I thought you couldn't swim?" Holly said, and Callous snorted, thinking of all the lives Clevenger had drifted through, drowning time and time again.

"I still can't. I went under as soon as we fell through. Took in a lungful, and that was it. It was the shortest life I've ever lived."

"Wait—when you fell through, you were alive?" Bigs and McCallan might have said it together, Holly wasn't sure, but the sentiment rang true for both. They weren't sure if they were dead or alive, of what path they trudged now.

"Well, you're both not alive, I can guarantee that. I was alive because I finally thought of someone else for once, when I pushed him through. He wasn't going to make it till my friend and I helped," and he patted Callous. "No, he wasn't supposed to be there at all, in the Below." Clevenger pointed with his finger to the ground, and Holly glared at Bigs for sending him to that dry gulley to begin with.

"He was out of order," Bigs countered. "He gave parts away without knowing the etiquette, the import, the..."

"Balance. Yes, always the balance with you. Why do you think we gave him back his eyes and heart to begin with?"

Bigs and McCallan looked at each other and considered the obvious sign they'd missed at the trial.

"I wouldn't have given him anything if I wasn't sure he was balanced to the right. And now I know by dying, by being here and not blown to ash, that I am, too. Look at me," he said, as he wiped the tears from his cheek. "I finally died the right way." Clevenger sighed with the knowledge of it all, and Callous was so moved, he pressed his long face toward Clevenger and held it against the man he'd rode beneath for eons. "My body got tangled on the rapids at Point of Rocks. Just another anonymous drowning to them, when they pulled me up. But I was already on the towpath watching and knew something was different this time. *That I was here.* That I wasn't sent back to the gulley. I finally knew I'd done it, in helping him through. Of course, they didn't know me, so no one has said my name. You shouldn't either, till I'm ready."

A man and woman on a tandem bicycle rode toward them, coming down from Harpers Ferry, and so they all fell silent—the living and dead—until the man and woman rode awestruck and disbelieving right through the center of the towpath. Their jaws slack. Their eyes disbelieving in not only seeing the candlelight Nora carried, but dead men walking with a mule, all dripping river water to the dusty towpath.

"And Edison?" McCallan said, once they were alone again. He looked at Clevenger, because the man held some certain knowledge that sparkled now on his skin. He was so close to the calling, so close to hearing his name one last time, to being lifted up, he practically brimmed with a joyous comprehension of the living world. Looking across the water, he lingered now and sniffed the air as the scent of lilac and blueberry carried to him and a lilting birdsong strummed in the high treetops. Even the train trestle hummed beside them. Nora looked and heard voices on the river not far off amidst a thunder of echoing oars. Refocusing on the candle, she knew it was starting all over again. The light was bringing unto it whomever was in need, and they wouldn't have much more time alone.

"Edison must have entered out of turn," Clevenger said. "Did something he touch come before him? Some object he held close?"

"The ring. The true ring." Holly, Bigs, and McCallan spoke in unison, and Nora's ring pulsed at mention of the other one. A shock of warmth raced through her finger, and she hid her hand behind her back.

"Once it crossed into the living realm, he gave up any claim he had on staying," Clevenger added. "The ring replaced him. When he fell through, he was but an echo, a shadow swept aside. It didn't help that he fell right through that silver stream either," and he pointed at the cauldron Miss Misery carried, before she turned to the railroad track.

"It's going to stop right here." Pointing beside them, the sound of a train clattered nearby. In another hundred yards a tunnel went through the mountain, crossed the Potomac on a trestle, and curved into Harpers Ferry. "I suggest we get ready to ride."

The man and woman on the bicycle had returned. Another dozen people had gathered on the towpath with them. The river also churned with the sound of oars and shouts, and out of the blinding sunlight, reflected on the surface, five boats appeared. One had the sheriff and two officers in it. Holly could still feel their hands on his foot. He shook his left leg out; it was heavy and seemed to get heavier the closer the officers approached.

"Well, friends," Clevenger said, and patted Callous, before stepping back to the canal, away from a footbridge. Old wooden slats creaked beneath the rest of them as they hurried across. The steel tracks screeched just a few yards off. The conductor's face was slack as he brought the full weight of a thirty-car coal train to a stop just to watch the candlelight. "Things seem to be coming to a bit of a head," Clevenger noted. "Now might be a good time to say my name."

39

THE CROWD COULDN'T MOVE WHEN THEY SAW IT. The sheriff and his men were just as dumbstruck by the sudden swirling rush of wind. Nora, Holly, Callous—everyone—had hurried across the footbridge and climbed aboard a flatbed right behind the engine, all of them helping Callous climb up. Then Nora was whispering to the conductor. Telling him about the candle and where they needed to go—to the Harpers Ferry train station—when Callous snorted, and Holly knew it was time. "Clevenger!" he sang out, and the first burst of wind appeared. A vortex of dust and leaves swirled around the smiling man, as a siren pierced the whole valley, echoing in waves above it. Holly knew it wasn't much longer for Clevenger. Time was different inside the calling, considering he'd experienced it once before, but didn't know that listening was perhaps the most important thing about it. But the moment, he recalled, had stretched on and on. There'd been nothing fixed in his mind to mark the minutes and hours and days that flowed through him. The same sensation must have engulfed Clevenger now. As for everyone else, it was over in a second.

"Oh!" Someone on the towpath cried out, and that was it. The siren stopped pulsing above the valley. The vortex of dust and leaves floated down, scattering across the towpath. Even the sheriff and his men had been able to bring their boat to the banks in the sudden silence and step ashore. But the train had already shuddered to a start. Rumbling to life, the engine moved slowly at first, before the momentum of it shook through each subsequent car. Then they were rolling away from the whole scene, rumbling toward Harpers Ferry, entering a dark tunnel.

"You still have your ring?" Holly spoke; Nora was in front of him by only five feet now. He saw the candlelight. Its small beacon grew larger in the tunnel, expanding so that they could all see each other in the silvery glow. There was still a barrier between Holly and Nora, but they could feel it subsiding, as if they were getting closer to where they needed to go. Holly saw how the tracks followed a subtle curve here, cutting through the mountain. But he couldn't see the bright opening yet, or the bridge that would carry them into Harpers Ferry and the station.

"I do," Nora said. "I wouldn't take it off for anything."

"I'm sorry I gave mine away. I didn't mean it."

"To that man who got blown to ash?"

"It was a kind of bribe, I think. All so I could get into his place." Holly nodded at Bigs, who smiled at Nora and bowed, and it was all so ridiculous: a dead man introducing his living wife to another dead man. Holly had to laugh at the whole absurd scene.

"Madame, I am enchanted."

"Likewise." McCallan bowed as well, but kept his hand the whole time on Callous's rump, as did Bigs.

"I think you can let go now." Miss Misery had watched and was mumbling something and tracing her lips. She figured her separation spell was still working, though diminished—as that had been cast over a day ago—and she'd since counteracted it with the binding spell at the confluence with the cauldron. Yet, throughout all this, Francis was all she could think about. In just hearing Nora and Holly's obvious love, in feeling it work against the invisible separation, it had her thinking about Francis and why he was attracted to her. She didn't need Holly's passion anymore. Was convinced of it, and had just finished a spell that she was sure would dissolve the rest of the barrier. Stepping toward Holly, she could feel it dissolving, held her hands up in the air and wet her lips, and was determined to kiss him right then and there—to give him back his passion—when Nora stepped in front of her.

"It's alright," Nora said, and placed her hand on his wet, dripping arm. Now that she'd touched him, as easy as that, he leaned down to her, his new blue eyes mesmerized by her beauty. The candlelight carved silvery shadows and glints in her cheeks and hair, and he traced each amber wave with his hand. A green spark crackled between their lips before they kissed—and then—*silence*. Moments lasted and fell and died. He saw the racetrack. Felt horses churning beneath him. Felt air rushing past. Saw her sitting at the kitchen table, smiling, sunlight blazing in the window above the sink. And she was singing to someone he couldn't see. Someone was singing with her. *And she was happy!*

"Goodness." Juney watched the long, quiet kiss and then smiled after realizing she was giggling watching them. Then she touched Nora's back. Nora was about to drop the candle, and without missing a beat, Nora handed the candle to Juney. As Nora leaned back from Holly, they all watched as a silver thread unspooled from Nora's lips for a foot and a half before Holly pinched it off and ate up the gossamer cord, swallowing it whole.

"I don't want to take all of it now. You've still got to live."

Nora traced her lips and leaned against Holly and watched the growing light now that the end of the tunnel had appeared. The bridge's trestles glinted in the sun as Harpers Ferry showed on the other side of the Potomac. They'd be at the station in a few minutes. Juney had already moved to where she could hold the candle behind the conductor. He leaned out of his window to look back at it, and she said something to him, and he nodded his head. "She's something, isn't she?" Nora said.

"She reminds me of you," and Holly smiled when he said it.

"She's got gumption, that's for sure. And a level head."

"And she's not afraid to help."

"What do you think she hears in the candle?" Bigs had stepped closer to their conversation; McCallan had leaned in, too. They'd both taken their hands from Callous and were ready to hold onto Holly at the slightest hint they might be reduced to ash.

"I think it's what everyone hears—what they need." Nora looked at him and was about to say something, but the train whistle blared with a short burst once, twice—before letting out a long, echoing blast—and the river shimmered beneath them as the train came into the clear air. Bigs shivered and held onto McCallan, their pants and jackets dripping wet. In the relative quiet after the train whistle stopped, Nora asked what she'd wanted to know from the dead man. "What do *you* hear in it?"

Bigs was quiet. The trestles thudded beneath them. He looked down and saw the water and remembered Savannah. 1864. General Sherman's march to the sea. How he'd been back in another life, having bartered for it with a particularly fresh liver he'd come across. There'd been a woman he'd gotten to know in just the few weeks he'd been there. She owned a saloon and all he'd wanted was to sip his julep and watch the Savannah River glint in the sunlight. "Just like this," he muttered, remembering it all before Sherman came through. Before Miss Clarabell went away. West. To Denver, he recalled. He wandered around a bit after that. But in Texas, a cheat at a card game was a faster draw. He still had the bullet hole after he was shot on the banks of the Brazos, tumbling into the muddy depths. It hadn't killed him, of course, the bullet, but the water had. He got another heart almost at once after he came back up, but he'd never found his true object. The one thing to help him ascend to the next level. So he'd designed the saloon in the Above just like the one in Savannah. To remember. And he always hoped Miss Clarabell might have drowned somewhere, too, so he might meet her again.

"What do you hear?" Nora repeated.

"I hear this," Bigs recalled. "The water lapping the rocks. The sunlight. It has a sound, too. Just like the candle. But I also hear a banjo. A fiddle tune. A woman's long-hemmed dress sweeping the wooden floorboards. Sawdust crunching beneath her heels."

The train had slowed and turned north as the dusty station came into focus. Leaning out to look, they all heard the whistle blast again before the big thundering weight of all those railcars came shuddering to a stop.

"Well, I hope you find her." Looking at Bigs, Nora touched his arm. "But we still have a situation here." She pointed at Juney, who was already scrambling off the flatbed. Juney was hollering at them and holding up the candle. She was trying to bring as many folks as she could to the tracks.

"What in the world?" Holly couldn't understand what she was doing. Why was she *bringing* attention to them, when slinking away was the right play? But Nora tugged his shirt, and he knew. The girl was smarter than all of them. The sheriff was already standing in the parking lot. His gun at his side.

40

"HOW THE HELL DID HE BEAT US HERE?" Holly pointed to the police car in the parking lot; its blue and red lights flashed as a crowd gathered.

"Well, I suppose it wasn't the *fastest* train." As Bigs spoke, he helped Callous jump down from the flatbed. McCallan had already jumped down and was kneeling on the tracks—his right ankle had popped loose.

"I'm okay, if you're wondering. But walking might not be an option from here on out." McCallan held out his hand, and Bigs pulled him up and slumped him against Callous. The mule sighed and shook his head to intimate that the man should just jump up already. Bigs understood, as did Holly, and they helped McCallan atop the mule. "Well," McCallan said, as he leaned against the mule's sturdy neck, considering he'd never rode before. "This should be interesting."

"Just ease yourself against him. Find the rhythm of it," Holly instructed.

"No, I mean—there's another mule—and it's coming this way." McCallan pointed across the tops of the heads murmuring about the candlelight, and Nora could see Mercy trotting toward the station.

"Mercy!" Nora had already caught up to Juney, but didn't take the candle. "You're okay with it?" she said, nodding at the steady flame.

"I'm just about as okay as I've ever been," and Juney smiled at Nora with a bright, mischievous grin.

"Then I've got to grab Mercy." The mule was running toward Nora, and some of the crowd screamed as they parted to let the beast run through. Nora held up her hand, and Mercy stopped before her, but looked at Callous the whole time. They were an inverse image of each other. Callous larger and mostly dust-colored, a blonde bordering on bleached gold. His big, brown, cracked teeth showed, as if smiling for Mercy. The girl mule was a dark, rich umber, with white splashes on all her hooves like she were wearing knit socks. She stood a few inches shorter and

175

shook her head back and forth as if to tell Callous they had some work to do first before any courting could commence.

"That had to be one of the slowest getaways I've ever seen. I'm here to talk about the girl." Sheriff Bay waved his hand at Juney, now that Mercy had parted the crowd, and he could see her. He was about twenty feet off, and when he began to walk toward the edge of the crowd, Juney took it upon herself to hold the candle up higher. In a moment, the crowd flowed back to fill the gap Mercy had made, and the sheriff was stuck again on the outside looking in.

"It's just like Savannah all over again, isn't it, when Sherman came through." Bigs shook his head and touched Mercy. He'd stepped closer to Nora, before shivering when he saw the ring Nora still had on her finger. The things he could barter for with that. He wouldn't have to pass judgement on the others like he had all this time. He could leave the saloon to someone else. Someone incomplete and hungry like he'd been. Hearing all his thoughts, Callous snorted and then whinnied at him, and Bigs understood.

"But I didn't think Savannah ended too well for you?" McCallan looked down at Bigs.

"Sure it did. We *negotiated* is what we did. Not a shot was fired. A few of us rode out ahead. A distraction is what it's called in military circles. And I propose we do the same here. To give them some time." Bigs nodded at Nora and patted Holly's shoulder. Jumping then in one motion, he was atop Mercy and moving with her toward Callous.

"Be careful." Miss Misery had stepped toward them, her hands combining the last of the herbs and tinctures she'd brought. She then muttered a phrase none of them understood and touched Mercy's face, holding her a second.

"What's the worst the sheriff can do," Bigs said to anyone who'd listen, "kill us again?"

"Take the candle." Handing it up, Juney smiled at the men. And after Bigs and McCallan stared briefly at the light—with Bigs hearing again that fiddle tune and Miss Clarabell's dress sweeping the floorboards—they started out, riding in a wide circle around the crowd.

"I didn't think he."

"How can we still be."

"Are there any other ones besides the one he."

The crowd cried out and was stunned to see the light moving around them in a circle. The sheriff tried to reach up and grab it every time Bigs and Mercy galloped past, but he couldn't stop them. He'd already put his gun away, worried he might shoot one of the folks following the light. It was all so dizzying and confusing that the first bright explosion only brought more of an urgency to the moment. Miss Misery's cauldron bubbled with a green light and sent up flares of brilliant, bursting stars above the station. Nora nodded at Holly and Juney and they were off, moving toward the river. Miss Misery followed and was muttering as they walked to where Harpers Ferry ended and the Potomac and Shenandoah met. The sheriff's boat was there. A small motor was in back. Holly had already pulled the cord and sat in the stern as Nora and Miss Misery pushed off. Maneuvering them below the rapids at the confluence, he shivered to think he'd died beneath those same rocks. Touching his arm, Nora steadied him as he brought the boat across to where she'd sat with the candle. It was where Juney had first found him, tugging on his wet hand. Now Ruddy was standing there when they arrived.

"You're the boy I gave my heart to." Holly stared in disbelief as the boy smiled.

"My daddy ain't never been better. Thanks again. I was out here fishing this morning. Saw it when the sheriff and those other boats went across. I could just tell it was about you."

"We're going home, Ruddy," Nora said. "We don't need the cave this time. But could you do us a favor?" and she pointed at the boat, and Ruddy understood.

"They won't know where you are. I'll ride on down to Brunswick if I have to. It's the least I could do."

Ruddy pointed to a trail behind him in the brush and Nora knew it would take them up winding to the road—then across it. It was just another mile up along the ridge. They'd be home before Bigs and McCallan even stopped riding in circles by the station. *Home.* Her body ached to be there. To see the oak tree. The strawberry bush. Just so she could watch Holly again in the kitchen. Maybe he'd reach up to one of his old whiskey bottles? Maybe he could stay a while longer? Maybe he didn't have to go?

"You okay?" Holly held her arm. Ruddy had already sped off, and as they started up, the trees and brush hid them, and it was cooler under the shadows as they walked in single file toward the swooshing sound of cars going by on the roadway.

"I feel like I've just gotten you back. And now..."

"Now we're going to where I have to leave again. I know . . . It's all happening so fast." Holly held her close as they waited till it was clear. Then all four of them scampered across and found the trailhead on the other side and were about to start up when a car honked at them, before pulling over to the shoulder. A man stared from behind the wheel. Pointing at the trees, he shouted above the engine noise, but Miss Misery already had her hands up and was walking toward him.

"Francis, we're almost there. Did you talk to him? Is he coming? Because it's got to be tonight."

41

HOLLY AND NORA WEREN'T SURE WHAT MISS MISERY meant by what she'd said to Francis, the friend who'd lent Holly the rowboat to begin with. They just kept following Juney up, even as they looked back now and then to see if Miss Misery was behind them—but they couldn't see her anywhere. Their home wasn't far off, and Holly felt lighter already, even though his dripping boxer shorts and undershirt sopped with each step. "Maybe I could grab a suit?" he said, and touched Nora's arm.

"I rather like you this way," she said. "At least I know you don't have any place to hide a whiskey bottle," and she nudged him with her elbow, and they both smiled to remember some of his more lubricated nights.

"I thought you liked it when I drank."

"I liked it when *we* drank—but that happened less and less." She stopped. He was quiet and his legs dragged when he thought of the agony he'd put her through, drinking so much those last few months before he died. "But I'm not going to be mad at you now. Not when you've come back somehow. I don't want to send you off by saying the wrong thing."

"You could never be wrong about me."

"Oh, sure I could." She held both his hands now and looked at him. Juney was already gone; she'd walked on ahead past a clump of trees, and then it was just the two of them alone in some impossible way, after the last few days. "I never thought I could do this again—hold your hands. I didn't know life went like this."

"And how is life?"

"Right now, it's sideways."

"Or upside down."

"I haven't slept in ages." Nora yawned, and Holly touched the back of her head, pressing her cheek to his shoulder.

"Well, don't sleep now. That could be it. You might sleep for days and who knows where I'll be."

"You'll be in the tree. Always."

"I'll be in the tree. You know that's where we're headed, right?"

She leaned back from his wet shoulder and smiled. Touched her heart to show him. "I felt it in here ever since you left. Knew somehow you'd done something wrong, even in death. Of course."

He looked at her, and they laughed.

"You always had to make things difficult, didn't you?"

"Well, you've got to break a few eggs, don't you? What's the saying?"

"To make an omelet, stupid."

He smiled and all his perfect teeth seemed to glow in the shade beneath the tree as she kissed him. Breathing in his leather saddle-whiskey-apple pie scent, she wanted to hold him forever. But felt her body moving even then, even as she held him. The house wasn't but another hundred yards. Juney was probably getting something ready, sweeping or lighting a candle or doing something smart and warm and useful. The afternoon had gotten cloudy all a sudden, and as they came through the trail to the lower yard, she could see the house lit up. The front windows were open, and the curtains billowed out as a fresh breeze shook the ridge. She felt like she hadn't spoken to him in years about anything and now here he was, and she couldn't think of a thing to say—other than to tease him about his drinking.

"You don't have to."

"What?" She stared at him.

"Say anything. You don't have to. I'm the one who has to apologize. It was what I wanted to do the other night, when I saw you. You were waiting for me and worried I hadn't come home yet. You knew I was dead, but wouldn't admit it. Inside though, you were sure; I could tell."

She nodded and wrapped her arms around her chest standing there. Remembering the night she swept the dust into a pile, and he'd dropped the candle and metal clasp and bird's nest before her. *The bird's nest.* She still felt it in her stomach changing things, its energy vibrating through her, rushing out and out. Because always when she looked inside, she saw the oak tree. Remembered looking up as the night spun back. and Holly seemed pulled into a blanket of stars.

"I saw some things, Nora. Some of the things I've been judged by. And even if I wasn't entirely in the wrong, I need to tell you about them. And about something I did. With Miss Misery."

"Oh, I know. You kissed her. Or rather—she kissed you. I know all about it. I could see it on your lips. And hers. It's okay. Truly."

"That's not it. Not hardly," and he stopped a moment just to look at her. Just to remember what she looked like before he had to tell her what he knew he had to say. "When I was younger. When we were kids and you served me root beer floats and I worked the shed row at the track."

"What about the track?" Her mind was telescoping back. She was standing there on the edge of the yard, but she was seeing something else. She saw herself at the soda fountain as soon as Holly mentioned root beer floats. She was younger. The dress she wore came down to her knees. The smell of vanilla was always in the air, chocolate syrup on her hands. *The man.* The stupid businessman she'd slept with. Who'd lied to her even though she didn't mind being lied to as long as she was able to do it with someone—*with anyone*—to know what it was like to be loved. To give yourself over completely, but then to realize only later she didn't have to rush into being a woman, into growing up. But you always realize that too late. Everyone does. It's always too late to go back. But there she was. She saw Holly sitting at the counter. The root beer float in front of him, and that man—*that stupid man*—was talking to him. How had she forgotten? She was probably working instead, lining up more floats and ice cream cones, when he pulled Holly aside, whispered about something, nodding all the while, smiling his sick city-slicker smile.

"Miss Misery worked the shed row then. I'd forgotten all that she'd done until I had to watch it all over again, with the powders and packets of herbs and tinctures she made for the horses. She could tell who'd win, too, some nights. I bet on some of those tips. But that's not what I have to say about it."

"And what is it you have to say?" Her voice was sharp and cut Holly. He could feel her body stepping back from his. Could feel her love retreating, protecting her.

"She made a certain mixture. A special one. For women with a particular *condition*," and he touched a wet hand to his belly as he said it.

"No. *No*," she said, and touched her belly just as he had.

"Yes, I have to say it. You have to hear it from me before I go. Herbs to be mixed and taken down with bitter water."

She saw the stupid businessman smiling as soon as he said it. Saw the night he brought her the packet of herbs. The bottle of seltzer water he said would make it easier on her stomach. The fizzy water she drank down as she watched him. Considering she wanted to please him. Wanted to still be with him because she thought it was love when it wasn't. When she wasn't sure what she was doing. What she was giving up. No one ever does.

"I didn't know it was for you. I swear. He told me I'd be a jockey. That he had investors lined up, speculating on the track. That I was their man."

"*You?*" and she stepped back, her mouth hard and dark. "You took my child from me? You were the one that helped? With that . . . *woman*?"

"I didn't know, Nora. I swear, I didn't."

But she was gone. She'd turned as soon as she knew it was true. As soon as she felt it in her body that her husband had bought the potion she'd taken all too willingly to have it off. To shed the life inside her. The only chance she'd had. *The tree!* She had to see the tree. To see if there was some way she could burn it or chop it down. Some way to keep him here to yell at and to curse as long as it took to make it right. Her love. Her Holly. Her child.

42

HOLLY HURRIED AFTER NORA BUT ONLY GOT as far as the front driveway. Nora had rushed around back, and all he could see was a dark Chrysler Phaeton parked there. The car was magnificent and sleek. The top was down, and a man sat at the wheel as the radio played. A soft medley of clarinets and trumpets eased off into the air. *Lamenting.* The music was lamenting some passing away. Some lost love or decision, and he felt it all too well in his soggy bones and had a mind to tell the man to quit it, when he recognized him. It was a man he'd seen before. Long before. Yet stepping closer, he wasn't prepared to watch Mr. Gettys stand up from the driver's side and step into the yard. "You look . . . well," Mr. Gettys said. His slick auburn hair close and neat. His green piercing eyes trailing over Holly's dripping boxer shorts and undershirt.

"You can see me?"

"Of course, I can. I've been waiting all this time. Francis mentioned something to me in passing and then I just found my way here, even though I've never seen the place. There was something drawing me. Something pure. Something . . . I need."

"And what's that?" It'd been years since he'd caught Holly and Josiah cheating with their loaded dice.

"Me." Miss Misery stood behind them. Francis was still in his car. They'd driven up and parked beside the Chrysler without Holly noticing. He'd been so captivated by Mr. Gettys and the gravity he still held over him, the rest of the world had dissolved. But now that Miss Misery stepped closer, the sounds of the world came crashing back. He heard Juney somewhere inside the house, her high-pitched voice calling for something. Nora was hitting something, too. Chopping with the axe. *The tree!* He could feel each whack she took resound in his belly. Like she was hacking at his own arms and legs. He turned to go, but Mr. Gettys was there, and Miss Misery was staring into the man's cold, green eyes, and Holly couldn't budge.

"You're here because you've had some bad luck," she said. "I heard all about the tables, how the old magnetic coils don't work so well anymore. You've even lost your touch at the private tables."

Smiling, the faintest flush had risen in his cheeks. "Misericordia, always a pleasure to hear how perceptive you are."

"And you haven't aged a day since I first started, when I worked the shed row. When I had the names of the winners whenever I wanted. How I gave them away for peanuts back then, I was so stupid. But now you want some names, some winners again. And your senses brought you here. To me. You think I can help with one big score at the track, and all your troubles will vanish?"

"That's about the gist of it. I do commend your powers of summation."

"Wait. You can tell the future?" Francis had come up beside Miss Misery and placed a hand on her shoulder. She didn't say anything, but nodded, and he shook his head in wonder at the woman he would walk over broken glass for just to be near.

"But you left the track, didn't you?" Mr. Gettys continued, looking right past Francis. "You went back to your woods and tinctures. I've kept tabs all this time. You never know when someone with your . . . skillset might come in handy. I always thought it was too bad about Eddie T."

"Don't you say his name!" Miss Misery's cheeks flared with silver sparks. As she stepped closer to him, the wind and clouds swirled higher, darkening the ridge.

"I always did enjoy his company. He lost so consistently, I believe he owed me more than anyone before he passed."

Holly could feel Nora swinging the axe, swinging against the tree, but couldn't move. He wanted to stop her. To tell her he hadn't known about the pregnancy, and to even bring Miss Misery with him to apologize and explain. But as Mr. Gettys leaned back against his car, with Miss Misery leaning closer, he wasn't sure what she might do now that he'd brought up Eddie T., and the love she'd lost.

"I never did collect from him. So I thought you might be persuaded to help, when I heard."

"Heard what?" She was taller than him by an inch, and Francis didn't know what to do as she loomed closer.

"Heard you'd hypnotized poor Francis here. Someone who also frequents my parlors. What did you use, a love potion? Another one of your bestsellers?"

Touching her lips, Miss Misery felt Holly's passion inside them and turned to Francis. She'd wanted to keep it for herself once she'd found Holly in the woods those days ago. She'd wanted it like never before. And when Francis had seen her, and loved her completely, she reveled in the sensation of being loved again. Of being desired. But was it her? *And was it real?*

"Now, wait a second." Francis pointed a finger at Mr. Gettys. "I haven't been hypnotized by anyone. And anyway, that's none of your goddamn business."

"Everything's my goddamn business."

"Francis?" Miss Misery kept her eyes on her love, but pointed a wicked finger at Mr. Gettys so he couldn't move an inch from his car. But she had to know. "Francis, what do you see when you look at me?"

There was a thudding sound, and Holly could feel Francis, could hear inside him now. He could feel the man's heart pounding louder to be so close to Miss Misery and to hear the hurt in her voice, the doubt.

"I see you, of course. What do you mean?"

"No. What do you *see*?"

The trees stopped swaying. Holly watched a single bluebird alight on a high branch. Hovering, the clouds had paused in their passage. Even Nora must have stopped chopping. The last thudding axe blow echoed like a hollow drum, and then ceased.

Closing his eyes, Francis spun a bit before he spoke, his arms outstretched. "I see an open field. A meadow. I see sunlight and dandelions drifting in the breeze. I see your front porch, too. The radio at twilight. You're sitting beside me with the doors open. We're listening to music and to each other. You are music, if you can understand. It's both somehow. Somehow, you move up in the air, but also shine beside me. Always."

Miss Misery let out a loud breath once Francis stopped. The ridge was quiet. Even Mr. Gettys seemed awed by hearing Francis speak his sprawling love into being.

"Then you won't mind if I do this." And leaning in all the way, Holly saw the eerie green sparks flash from Miss Misery's lips, as she kissed Mr. Gettys.

43

MR. GETTYS HAD TO KNEEL IN THE GRAVEL driveway as Miss Misery's passion poured into him for the full thirty seconds she kept her lips pressed to his. Francis was dumbstruck to see it, and Holly had to hold him back, breaking a rule he didn't think he could. Considering the dead couldn't touch anyone who hadn't touched them first. But he didn't feel so much dead now as in-between life and death. There was something moving in him, rising up like the wind now with the leaves that spiraled in a bursting vortex, scattering across the yard. Nora had commenced chopping again, and each blow thundered through him with such weight, he wondered if the portal of the tree was now imbedded in him, because he knew that was where he was meant to go. But he couldn't understand why she would want to chop it down? He held onto Francis, and even wondered if he should bring up the smashed boat he borrowed from him, the one he drowned in, but thought better of it. Miss Misery was turning to face them—for all at once—she'd changed.

Before, she'd been a smoother, softer version of the wild woman of the woods. But something had reverted in her now that the passion had unspooled from her in its silver thread. So that instead of holding Francis back, Holly had to hold him up. Her hair was kinked up again, and a few leaves even fluttered down as if by habit to land in the nest of her tangled waves. Her dress—so stylishly fitted to her full hips before—was now wrinkled and rubbed by some imperceptible soil. And if it wasn't quite burlap, the richer velvet material had reverted somewhere close to it. Holly wanted to touch the fabric to test it, but feared what other transformation the woman might still complete.

"What do you see now?" She still had a strength to her; that was obvious. As she moved away from Mr. Gettys, Holly let go of Francis and watched as she leaned

186

down to help him stand to face her. Her plump, full lips had subsided to a thinner pair of cracked, peeling shapes. To believe it all, Francis even reached out to trace the lips himself, moving his finger along their ragged outline. He touched her cheek, too. Shaded not by rouge or whatever internal flame had lit her before, but by a shadow of dirt and caked-on dust. "It's the earth," she said. "It's what I work in; it's what I work with. Kneading it. Sowing it. Shaping it with all the herbs and tinctures I craft. After all that work, it becomes you. This is the real me. It was only the passion I took from Holly before that lit me up like that."

"I see," and Francis nodded at the changed woman in front of him.

"*What* can you see?" Miss Misery touched his face, holding his chin.

For a moment, Francis looked off in the air above her, to the trees swaying in the breeze, and Holly and Miss Misery, and even the stunned and intoxicated Mr. Gettys had no idea what Francis might say. "I see our home. Not too far from here, so we can visit Nora. You might pull a couple names of horses that will win from your mind now and then. But I just let you write them on a piece of paper we burn up each night in the fire. The folks who come and want your gift, your voice to lead them through whatever toil or troubles they think will befall them, I keep away. I say to them, 'She's done. Sorry. Miss Misery is Misericordia now and forever, and she's mine. You can get your fortune somewhere else.'" Wrapping his arms around her, Holly heard her thundering heartbeat. She cried out once with a laugh, and then she was kissing Francis, and no green sparks emerged. No silver thread unspooled from either of them. But her miraculous lips did plump up again as a different, truer spark kindled inside her, illuminating her essence. Francis kissed her back, and they swayed in each other's arms even as Holly heard that thundering heartbeat racing louder—until it echoed across the ridge.

"I feel . . . different." Mr. Gettys stood beside Holly and touched his hands along his chest. Craning his neck to the left and right, he seemed to be resizing the fit of his skin. "What does it mean?" He looked at Holly, his eyes sparkling and lit from within. A look Holly had only ever seen in the man when he was wiping out some fool's life savings at one of his rigged tables. But Holly didn't have time to tell him. The thundering had grown louder, and a shouted cry sounded so raw and wild, he had to cover his ears. Callous and Mercy were galloping up the gravel drive. Bigs rode atop Mercy and held the candle and was singing some old Rebel tune. McCallan rode Callous and had an open whiskey bottle—gotten from God-knows-where on whatever path they'd taken to get here. They thundered into the yard and rustled up a circle of dust and scattered leaves before stopping beside Holly and Mr. Gettys. Holly looked and Miss Misery and Francis had disappeared into the house. Or the woods. Maybe that was best, he thought, for her to go off the same way he'd first encountered her—back to the woods and herbs and soil.

"Well, gents, I'd say we won't have to worry about the police for a while."

"We rode clear up to a cave above Harpers Ferry after rounding that parking lot. Must have been two miles. Had everyone roaring and chasing the light." McCallan nodded to the candle and took another swig of whiskey, and Holly had a mind to ask for a few swigs himself, but held back.

"The sheriff and another police car followed behind. A few other folks—transfixed by the candle—were in their cars. There were also a few on horses and wagons. It was a complete mess."

"A parade of fools, I'd say." McCallan wiped his mouth, and Holly could smell the smoky liquor, and without thinking, his arm reached up and his hand was on the bottle pulling it down.

"This one told us all about it." Bigs nodded at Mercy who snorted and shook her head, almost bashfully deferring the compliment. "In some way, I heard her just like I'm speaking now. It was remarkable. She said, '*Colonel John Mosby. A few miles north. A man on horseback can just squeeze through. Mosby hid his troops there, whenever the Union chased him.*' And sure enough, we squeezed through and heard the police yelling outside, and the other folks who followed were all hollering for the candle. But Mercy just kept us going until we came across a man and his three daughters, all living in a mine. In the prettiest little shed, if you can believe it. The girls were so happy dancing about when they saw Mercy, they put lilies around her neck." Holly hadn't noticed, but Mercy wore a braided necklace of yellow lilies.

"The man said he was partial to the dead, whatever that means. Said he'd gotten nothing but good things from them, and rubbed his chest. Said he knew who might like his last whiskey bottle, too, and handed it over." McCallan looked to his hand to show off the bottle, and blinked to see it was gone and that Holly was already tipping it back, taking one long, deep gulp.

"WELL, I THOUGHT IT WAS BACK." Juney had come from behind the house to stand by Holly. She reached up before Bigs could really tell what she was doing and stalked off with the candle.

"She's a determined one, isn't she?" Mr. Gettys smiled as he watched her leave. "I wonder..."

"Don't you do any wondering about her." Holly glared at Mr. Gettys and moved closer to him to make sure whatever passion he'd acquired didn't lend itself to the romantic type as far as Juney was concerned.

"I wonder how she'd do on a horse. She does have the perfect size."

"Horse?" Holly stopped. Felt the tears in his eyes. When he closed them, he could see a horse galloping on a track. Felt the breeze and rhythm of rising and falling—but he wasn't the one riding. He looked from somewhere high above to see Juney atop a blue roan. Juney guiding and teasing the horse along, asking for speed and getting it, before easing the horse off around the corners. Taking the cleanest line to the rail. "Listen, you already fooled me once about this, and it cost me my wife. Cost her the baby she always wanted. It sent Eddie T. out to get killed for nothing. Now you're going to start this all over again, dangling her a job as a jockey like you dangled before me?"

"I had every intention of giving you that job. But you didn't change the dice, did you?" Mr. Gettys twitched his thin auburn mustache, but seemed uneasy now as Holly jabbed a finger into his belly. The man didn't have the same pull over Holly as before. His power had eased out with all the passion pouring in from Miss Misery's kiss. He might have even meant what he said about Juney, about supporting her if she wanted to race. *A girl racing?* Holly thought, and smiled to know it was something Juney would probably grab ahold of even if Nora would think it too dangerous. But Nora would let her, he was sure. Nora would let her do anything, just as long as she stayed.

"You know, I actually believe you. You've changed. I just saw it for sure, and I imagine that's why Miss Misery brought you here—to kiss you—to give you some human decency after all these years. And it heartens me to see it. But there's something I've needed to do for a long while." Holly wanted to roll up his sleeves at that point, but remembered he didn't have any. He'd been standing in his dripping boxer shorts and undershirt this whole time, and instead handed the whiskey bottle to Bigs. "This is for Josiah and his wife Marlene—you son of a bitch." Pulling his right arm back like he'd never done on any man, Holly balled up his fist with such anger he felt his whole body condense into one coiled muscle, before he stepped with all his dripping weight into the punch.

It wasn't like he thought. The man's face was much softer and gave with a warmth to it that confused him. He'd closed his eyes right before punching, but when he opened them, he saw Callous standing before him, with McCallan looking down into the mule's distended side. Right where Holly's arm had disappeared. McCallan hiccupped, slapped his cheek to see it, as did Bigs, who slugged back another gulp of whiskey, as Holly—as confused as anyone—pulled from the mule's insides a perfect pink lung.

44

HOLLY KEPT REACHING IN FOR THE PARTS that Bigs and McCallan called for. They were not only drunk on whiskey, but the giddiness of finally trading in for the last parts they needed to ascend to the next level, wherever that took them. "Hell, I'd even like to get a new nose if that'd be alright?" Bigs slid his nose off and handed it to Holly who held it up for Callous to see. The mule snorted a strained affirmation, and Holly slid his hand into the mule's wobbly side, felt around for a nose, left the other nose inside, and pulled out a shorter boxy version that Bigs slapped onto his face with delight.

"It's perfect." McCallan was so moved in the changed countenance of his friend, he had to wipe a few tears from his cheek before calling out, "Teeth! A full set!"

Holly took the ones McCallan pulled out, leaving his face looking hollow and kicked in, before pulling out the prettiest little set McCallan had ever seen. Replacing them, he smiled before biting down with a chomping sound as Mr. Gettys looked on in disbelief.

"What the hell is in this whiskey?" He looked down because he'd taken the bottle from Bigs when the dead men began trading and replacing parts. Taking another swig, the man then sniffed the bottle, thought better of continuing down that path, and scurried off to his Phaeton. Holly looked at him once before he sped off down the long driveway, for there was something so much softer in the man now, Holly almost felt repulsed by him, and he wondered how long it might last. How many debts might he forgive, even when he needed the money now for his own troubles? But after reaching in and replacing the parts Bigs and McCallan clamored for, Holly stood in a daze as Mercy snorted to see it all unfold, before trotting closer to Callous. The mule was obviously exhausted, having his inventory rifled through like that, and Mercy nuzzled his snout, hoping to help fortify him in these efforts.

Oh, it was necessary, Callous said to her, as Holly could hear the whole exchange unfold. *I didn't need to see anyone being punched, so I just sidled over as easy as could be.*

You're so understanding, Mercy added.

Where I come from, this is old hat. The ones who can go higher have to be whole. That's part of the balancing. There's a whole balancing act going on.

It sounds ridiculous.

Well, I wouldn't say it isn't. It's just how it's all set up. And sometimes—now mind you, I've only heard this from the Fourth Judge of the More-Troubled Drowned Dead, the judge before me—that there is a clearing out now and then. A relinquishing of responsibilities, and a removal of those set up in positions of judgment and accord.

A clearing out, you say?

I've never seen one before or been in the midst of one, but I feel like I am now.

And what does that mean for you?

Holly watched as Mercy leaned back from nuzzling Callous to flutter her beautiful long lashes.

I'm not sure. I'm . . . different than them. I've been up there for so long, I don't know what will happen next. If it means I'll stay or go.

I do hope you'll stay.

So do I.

Holly knew how the mule felt. He patted Callous upon his distended side—which wasn't as distended anymore—and which he didn't even notice if he wasn't looking right at it. It was strange, he felt that way about all of them, all the dead men he'd seen and been around these last few days. Even in the cloud above the confluence. Everything seemed to dissolve the closer you looked at it, and he wondered if he was the same way. Was that why Nora got so angry? She was looking deeper inside me, and I had to tell her the truth, and sometimes the truth is too obvious to see.

There's only one way to find out. Callous was looking at Holly. So was Mercy. And Bigs and McCallan. All their eyes were focused on Holly, and he didn't feel like he was dissolving now that they were all focused on him. On the contrary, he felt inspected. Right down to the most infinitesimal molecule. But maybe it was the candle that was doing it, attuning them all alike. Aligning their visions and vibrations of being. He could hear it rise louder now that Mr. Gettys had rumbled away in his car. Now that Bigs and McCallan had stopped calling out for parts. And since the sweet voices of Mercy and Callous had subsided in his mind, there was only the dull thudding of Nora's axe rising to him. The thudding and thunderous swirl of some approaching judgement. A calling for him? For Bigs and McCallan and Callous? He wasn't sure. But stood motionless as he cocked his ear to listen as the rest of them looked at him once more, before moving off behind the house. All their eyes waiting, he could tell, waiting for whatever he needed to do next. For whatever his body demanded he do. But there was only the thudding axe. The axe chopping, thudding down. Nora surely grunting beneath the anger in her, the need to release whatever rage had built up over the years for the child she now knew Holly had helped keep from her in more ways than one.

"I'm afraid," he said to no one. There was no one there. The house looked on at him as he took a step closer. His body wasn't rushing him through whatever steps he had to complete. But there was something inside he knew he had to have, to hold, to bring to Nora. He couldn't go to her empty-handed after what he'd confessed. After what it meant to her and him, to their love. "*My wife,*" he whispered and watched the clouds gather, stacked up on top of one another above the ridge.

The mid-afternoon had vanished. The blue skies blotted out. It might as well have been twilight or later in the evening the way the light was pulled from the yard. "For the candle," he figured. "Maybe the candle is doing all this. For some ceremony. The one I missed, having given out my parts too early and too eager. The calling never had enough of me back then to be absorbed by, enough parts to sink into. Especially my heart." He touched his chest, and the thudding organ coincided with Nora's axe, and he slumped closer to the house and remembered the floorboards, and the sound of Nora sweeping the night he died. He had another whiskey bottle at least to offer his collection above the kitchen door. Another scent of himself to leave behind after he knew he'd be lifted up above the tree. Another offering to Nora and the house he'd never been able to fill with the life she wanted, the child. Her child. Their child. The one he knew she was lamenting now, and that he had to address in some way. Even though he had no earthly idea how that would go.

45

NORA WAS WEEPING WHEN HOLLY APPEARED. The axe she'd been using to destroy the oak was stuck in the side of it. A few fresh chunks of bark and moist woodchips were scattered atop the grass and beside the strawberry bush. Holly smelled the rich sap. Saw the axe still stuck in the side of the tree and his wife looking up where the higher branches shook and quivered with some disturbance just passed through them. Or marshaling its otherworldly strength again.

"They're gone," Nora said, not turning, not looking at him. Juney stood over her with the candle and frowned at Holly.

"Just like that," and Juney snapped her fingers and pointed to the sky.

"Bigs and McCallan?"

"They certainly were happy about it. But surprised, because I think it all happened too soon. They wanted to give you this. That man, Bigs, he must have had it in his jacket all along." Juney handed him something dark and smudged with black soot. Holly held it with some delicacy.

"My wedding ring?" He couldn't breathe. Couldn't move. Nora was about as stunned as he was and finally turned to watch him, tears lining her cheeks.

"I thought it was burned up in the cauldron?" Nora's voice was softer and raspy. She sounded like she'd been pulled through a fiery cauldron herself, with what Holly had told her about her unborn child, and he wanted nothing more than to touch her, to take all her pain. But he stayed back a few steps and held his folded-over jacket closer to his shirt. "I see you found your other suit. You look fine enough. Even if you're dead and dripping through it already."

Holly had found the suit in his closet like he knew it would be there and put it on with a shirt and tie and vest and the other pair of boots he kept for socializing. The ones he'd worn going fishing were his work boots and he wasn't too worried about losing them. But these ones he wanted to hold onto no matter what he had to go through next. "I always did like this suit better," he said, and rubbed the ring on a handkerchief he pulled from his vest pocket. "But my, I never thought I'd see this again."

"We just needed the silver from it for the potion. Just the color, which returned when you did. The ring was in the cauldron the whole time. Bigs must have seen it on the train." Miss Misery had appeared from somewhere behind the oak, stepping out of the underbrush, her hair a tangled mess, her dress smudged with clay and decorated with briars and prickers that must have stuck to it on her ambling walk home—from wherever she'd made off to with Francis. She also had the silliest grin on her face. The woman practically radiated warmth, and held up a small twisted, waxy shape in her hands.

"A bird's nest." Nora stood to see it, as if drawn to the shape she'd ingested before and which she credited with all the extraordinary impulses and intuitions she'd had since. "I didn't think you had any left."

"I was wrong. I had Francis drive me straight to the cave, or as close as we could get. It's not too far back from here. I had a feeling Juney would want it." Miss Misery stood closer so the girl could shine the candlelight on the intricate construction the swiftlets made. "Also, I thought you might like to meet one." Pulling from her dress a small velvet pouch, with the utmost care, Miss Misery reached inside the pouch and held a swiftlet in her hand. The bird looked from left to right before focusing on the candle and Juney. Then, in an instant, the bird hopped onto Miss Misery's palm, chirped once, and flapped its wings once before landing on Juney's left shoulder.

"My goodness. She's as light as cotton candy." Juney tilted her head the slightest bit and looked at her new friend, and smiled at Miss Misery for the gift.

"I can show you how to care for them, if you'd like. How to keep the cave warm. How to make the soup. How to be comforting when the rains come, and careful with the eggs."

Juney couldn't say anything; she just smiled and nodded her head.

"We all have animals in us," Holly said, knowing at once that was a rule. "And maybe you just found yours."

Mercy and Callous nodded to hear it and looked at Holly because they knew he was right, and also that time was almost up. Holly's time. It fluttered above the trees like a swiftlet, moving in and out of the shadows the clouds cast down, once a sudden breeze spiraled up and set a small vortex of swirling dust at his feet. But in an instant, it backed off. Nora was stepping through it, stomping through the current of it.

"No!" she cried, and her eyes fluttered from side to side. Her expression was wild; her hair spun out as she reached her arms up as if she meant to tackle the next vortex of wind and leaves, to keep her man here. "I'm not ready. You hear! I'm not!" Nora looked above the tree. This was where she knew she'd bury Holly, whenever she could finally bring herself to see his corpse at the police station. Where she'd give them all an earful and tell them right out in the open that Juney would never go back to that home. "Do you hear that! Never!" The clouds had fallen that much closer to the ridge. They seemed content to watch what would unfold next, and were edging in for a better look. "He can't go yet. Not yet." Nora's voice was softer and wan, and as she looked at Holly, she stepped toward the axe, but there was nothing left in her arms anymore. She'd been up for days, had traipsed along rivers, through mountains, up hillsides and cemeteries, and found out about her lost child. So instead of grabbing the axe, she yawned and looked at Holly. "You didn't know it was for me. You couldn't have."

"I never would have gotten them if I'd known," he said. "The herbs."

"And I know you didn't know either." Nora looked at Miss Misery who understood at once.

"That was the last time I ever agreed to mix that formula." Miss Misery stared at Holly, remembering the shed row and the young Hollis Pride looking into her eyes, a $50 bill in his hand.

"I helped Eddie T. gamble, Miss Misery. I was his friend."

"I've known that for years. You and I even spoke about it, though you probably can't recall. Sometimes I have that effect. Because it is just like a spider's web, this life, isn't it? Every strand leads to the next. And they all fold back on one another." She smiled, rubbed her face with a hand. She was looking up at the tree and sniffing something. Or seeing something she didn't want to describe yet. Something in the offing. Just on the other side of the next moment.

"Well, holy smokes, aren't either of you gonna hug or something? This is it, right?" Juney looked stunned as Holly and Nora just stood there—Holly dripping wet, Nora's exhausted body shaking now that another breeze had lifted—but it wasn't a vortex. There was still time.

"I'm not sure if I've done everything I needed to." Holly looked at the girl, then Nora. "I mean, what else do you need me to do!" He stared at the oak tree, then above it, into the swirling clouds. "I found the parts I gave away! Got new ones. I even helped a few pass on into some other place, up above where they were before. I think I helped some people." Holly looked at Miss Misery, and the woman smiled and stepped back from the tree. Callous and Mercy watched him, and kept their muzzles touching. "I mean, I can only think of one other thing I've wanted to do, but I didn't think it was something I'd have time for."

"What?" Nora wondered.

Unrolling the jacket he'd kept pressed against his side, Holly held two baseball mitts in his arm. "I kept these in my closet. All this time. I even have a ball. And after all these years, I just wondered, would you like to have a catch?"

NORA THREW HARDER THAN HOLLY THOUGHT. She even had some strange kind of loose grip on the ball because it knuckled coming at him, and he had a difficult time figuring out which way it would swerve as it approached. But after they'd thrown a few minutes, he'd gotten the rhythm of it. She was wonderful, his wife. She was strong and able, and he knew he could leave her now that he'd done something he'd refused her that first time they'd met. "Do you remember?" he said, and caught another swerving throw.

"I remember. I'd just come up from the creek, not too far off in Knoxville, by the church. I was playing there with Amy Sue Bishop and my cousin Josephine. We'd found all these sticks and stuck them in the mud like a dam, just to give the leaves some depth to run down to the river. I was visiting the whole summer. My folks were getting the place ready to sell in Bristol. Daddy had a chance at something in Smithsburg and wanted to live near Harpers Ferry. He always did like the water."

"You wore a blue knee-length dress with white butterflies on the sleeves. There were daffodils in your hair. I'd never seen you before when your cousin called your name." The ball smacked into Holly's glove, and he felt the leather, smelled the smooth surface of the ball. Felt the raised stitches.

"Josephine liked that boy you were with, Eric Carter Lee. She would have walked through fire to play ball with him."

"But I didn't let you." Holly looked at Nora. She held the ball and tossed it up to herself and caught it and nodded at the memory of it. The first shame Holly had felt returned to him, as he watched her understand it all. What he needed to regain. That feeling. After regaining everything else. Even as he was playing ball with her now, it still flooded back. The chance he'd lost back then of being with her for another moment. Of playing a whole game and watching her run the base paths, probably laughing the whole time. How he might have shown her how to swing a bat, choking up with her dusty hands. The moments he didn't have inside him, that he'd pushed away out of shyness or stubbornness or just plain stupidity. The shame was inside him again and raged up into his cheeks like flames before spreading along his neck. When it did, a thunderous crack sounded in the sky. A brilliant single bolt of lightning shivered down and touched the top of the tree, and a few branches splintered and exploded with a poof of smoke, and Juney shrieked to see it.

Running to Holly, Nora touched his arm, but he was already being swept up closer to the oak tree. The wind had risen, and a wide vortex appeared and swirled around the whole tree. It had gathered in the smoke from the exploded branches and the wood splinters, which spun in a furious circle that held Holly inside it, pulling him closer to the trunk.

"Holly!" Nora said his name. He hadn't heard it since he'd been back, and with her arm around Juney, the candlelight wavered and was taken up by the swirling vortex. A golden streak of light revolved around the middle of the whirling, smoky cauldron containing the tree and strawberry bush and Holly—who'd been pulled up to the first low-hanging branch. His legs were being raised up behind him and a siren sounded somewhere in the sky to mark the beginning of what he knew he had to hear.

"I love you!" he yelled, and knew in his body that his hands would let go any second. That it would be light, the calling. That it would pulse through him with a vibration that shook every last drop from his core. That the voice would call to him and him alone, and he had to listen this time until he was nothing but listening. Until all the years and thoughts and feelings collapsed into that single pulsing voice he had to hold onto tighter than anything he'd ever held. That even these events, these images of Nora and Juney and Miss Misery would divide into an endless fracture of color. That even color would hold no meaning. That he would just be riding on the voice like riding that blue roan on the track. That he would just be rhythm. Just rising and falling on the calling wave of sound. His sound. Alone.

Above it all. But before that. Before he let go. Before the calling washed over him and dissolved him and absorbed him in its lighted beauty, there was something his eyes needed to see. Something that was moving in Nora's apron—some silver force was pulsing with an intention that had Nora reaching into her pocket to feel the magnetic pull of the metal clasp she'd carried all this time and that Holly had given her and that he had no idea to its purpose. Until now.

"I love you!" Nora yelled back, as she held the clasp in the air. The clasp had opened, and a silver luminous thread unspooled from it. She shook it and the thread reacted as if on cue, unspooling like a lasso before being caught in the vortex, so that the thread spun around the tree and Holly, before somehow, the leading end of it shot back to her. Then Nora watched her own hand move toward the girl's belt loop. She could feel Holly's strong and capable—but still slippery—hands letting go even without looking. She was all eyes now in her mind. A thousand sparkling eyes had emerged from the depths of her body, so that she could see Holly, Juney, Miss Misery, Mercy, and Callous all at once. She could see the calling taking Holly up, even as the clasp was attached to Juney at her side, and she held the other end of the binding thread. And she wondered then, deep inside, what the calling would be for him this second time, when he could listen? When he had all his parts, and he'd done what it was he'd been called down to do. Now that he had his first shame back. The shame she'd forgiven him that night he first appeared. But what voice and what words and what language and what knowledge and what dreams and what forgiveness was he absorbing, even now as he slipped up into the rift above the tree? The stormy clouds had opened as she slapped the clasp down on Juney's belt loop. Her girl. Juney. Holly had done it. He'd given her a daughter after all.

Acknowledgements

As always, I'd like to thank my family for their continued support and encouragement. Without them, none of this would mean much, and I hope they know that.

I'd also like to thank all the talented writers, editors, artists and thinkers at April Gloaming Publishing. Their unwavering support helped bring this story to its finished form. The wonderful people at April Gloaming also seem to sense that there are many more stories embedded in the southern landscape, stories yet to be untold, and that this novel is just a precursor to a host of other characters and paths diverging and twining back together again. Just as the Potomac and Shenandoah Rivers do in their unending journey and rewriting of the land.

I'd also like to thank the wonderful readers I've been fortunate to work with – Jim McGrath and Jeanne Stafford; the notes they provided were invaluable in helping me clarify the world of this novel. I'm also indebted to Amity Bitzel, a onetime classmate whose own inventive writing helped spark an immersion for me in the underworld all these years later.

CHRISTOPHER K. DOYLE grew up in Brunswick, Maryland, a small town nestled on the banks of the Potomac River, B&O Railroad, C&O Canal and the Blue Ridge Mountains. After receiving his MFA at the University of Baltimore, he has written about the origin of country music, an embattled elementary school teacher, the C&O Canal, and the magical world of Harpers Ferry. He lives in Baltimore with his wife, daughter, and Rhodesian ridgeback, all in a cramped rowhouse.

Similar April Gloaming Titles:

*The House that Wasn't
There*
Andrew Forrest Baker

Ash Tuesday
Ariadne Blayde

Even in the Quiet Places
Christopher K. Doyle

*All Things Holy &
Heathen*
Chelsea Jackson

Postlude to the End Of
J. Parker Marvin

*The Peril of Remembering
Nice Things*
Jeffery Wade Gibbs

APRIL GLOAMING

View our full catalog at aprilgloaming.com